William D. Gallagher

Miami Woods

A golden wedding, and other poems

William D. Gallagher

Miami Woods
A golden wedding, and other poems

ISBN/EAN: 9783337721800

Printed in Europe, USA, Canada, Australia, Japan

Cover: Foto ©Andreas Hilbeck / pixelio.de

More available books at **www.hansebooks.com**

Miami Woods

A

GOLDEN WEDDING

AND

OTHER POEMS

BY

WILLIAM D. GALLAGHER

CINCINNATI
ROBERT CLARKE & CO
1881

Dedication.

TO

A MEMORY

SACRED FOREVER,

THIS VOLUME

IS NOW INSCRIBED.

APRIL, 1881.

When last the maple bud was swelling,
  When last the crocus bloom'd below,
Thy heart to mine its love was telling,
  Thy soul with mine kept ebb and flow:—
Again the maple bud is swelling,
  Again the crocus blooms below;
In heaven thy heart its love is telling,
  But still our souls keep ebb and flow.

When last the April bloom was flinging
  Sweet odors on the air of Spring,
In forest-aisles thy voice was ringing,
  Where thou with bird and brook didst sing:—
Again the April bloom is flinging
  Sweet odors on the air of Spring;
But now in heaven thy voice is ringing,
  Where thou dost with the angels sing.

APRIL, 1851.   (iii)

Preface.

Nearly the entire contents of this volume, preceding the Miscellaneous Poems, appear in print now for the first time, though written at various periods between twenty-five and forty-two years ago.

The Miscellaneous Poems herewith given to the public, are the productions chiefly of the author's earlier years, but make their first appearance now in a collective form.

In a subsequent volume will be embraced "The Ancient People," "Ballads of the Border," "Civile Bellum," "Monodramatos, the Reciter," "Lute and Lyre," and Miscellaneous Poems of later years.

Contents.

I.

𝕸iami 𝖂oods.

Well known to me is every alley green,
Dingle, and bushy dell, in this wild wood,
And every bosky bourn from side to side,
My daily walk, and ancient neighborhood.

MILTON: " Comus."

A solitary sorrow, antheming
A lonely grief.

KEATS: "Hyperion."

Proem.

Miami Woods!—What says the mighty Past,
To the still mightier Present, from the midst
Of all these vestiges of centuries gone,
That strew the plains and hills around?   I ask
The question thousands have thus asked before,
And get the common answer—echo!   Here,
Green on the crown'd acclivities, or dark
In the dim twilight of o'erarching trees
That clothe the valleys, we behold remains
Of human toil and triumph and dismay,
O'er which the oak that counts five hundred years
Spreads his protecting branches:—walls of earth;
Tlascalan gateways; sacrificial mounds;
The altars of a worship we know not;
And, beautiful in their silence, tombs of men
Who died before the parent tree had cast
The seed from which arose this hoary trunk,
That lies so low at last!   But though the eye
Meets these rude records, turn where'er it will,

They tell no story that is understood,
Of all the human love and hate and pride,
And all the joy, and strife and agony,
That once were known within these Sylvan homes,
So populous then, so void and silent now:
And vainly leans the listening ear to catch
A sound or syllable revealing more
Than these mute records to the eye disclose.

Pierce far into the depths of these old woods,
Where seem to meet the Present and the Past;
Hasten not hence, but with still lingering steps
Move to and fro; stand on the tumulus
That rises o'er a chieftain's ashes; trace
The circle and the square, which still remain
Distinct and beautiful; with reverent step
Approach the altar where of old were lit
The fires of sacrifice; snatch from its sleep
Of centuries, beneath the pregnant earth,
The sculptured image; and then question all.
—Question as well the winds, or waves! as well
The child that's with me here, as wise as I!
How silent, where a hundred tongues should speak,
If curiosity had but the power
To bid and be obeyed: how silent all!
There comes down from the Past no voice to tell
The tale so often asked.   The Present points

To these rude works alone, and they are mute.
E'en the high chambers of the tumuli,
In which were laid the bones of chiefs and kings
Who ruled here in the ages lost, withhold
The revelation sought.   The marvelous skill
And learning that in other lands have read
The secrets of the Past on images,
On stones, and on the corpses of the dead
Exhumed from the repose of centuries,
Read nothing here.   The garrulous tongue of Time
—Time, that has hung the forests round like clouds
Upon the hillsides: Time, that here has cut
Grooves in the rocks which antedate the pits
Hewn in the hills of Latium for the first
Foundations of old Rome,—throughout these wilds
Makes not a sign, and syllables no sound,
To break the eternal seal that rests on all!

So let it be!   Why seek to know what God,
In his inscrutable ways, has hidden thus?
It may be wise such mysteries to explore;
To probe the Past for what it holds so dark;
But in familiar things that lie along
Our daily walks, are lessons for us all:
And he who seeks the profit of his soul
In free communings with the things that speak

Most reverently of God on earth, may ask
The Present with humility, and find
In all about him revelations deep,
As I do now, here in Miami Woods.

𝔓art 𝔉irst.

1839.

THE autumn time is with us!—Its approach
Was heralded, not many days ago,
By hazy skies that veiled the brazen sun,
And sea-like murmurs from the rustling corn,
And low-voiced brooks that wandered drowsily
By pendent clusters of empurpling grapes
Swinging upon the vine.   And now, 'tis here!
And what a change hath pass'd upon the face
Of nature, where the waving forest spreads,
Then robed in deepest green!   All through the night
The subtle frost has plied its magic art;
And in the day the golden sun hath wrought
True wonders; and the winds of morn and even
Have touch'd with magic breath the changing leaves.
And now, as wanders the dilating eye
Athwart the varied landscape, circling far,
What gorgeousness, what blazonry, what pomp
Of colors, bursts upon the ravished sight!
Here, where the poplar rears its yellow crest,
A golden glory; yonder, where the oak
Stands monarch of the forest, and the ash

Is girt with flame-like parasite, and broad
The dogwood spreads beneath, and, fringing all,
The sumac blushes to the ground, a flood
Of deepest crimson; and afar, where looms
The gnarlèd gum, a cloud of bloodiest red ;
While, intermix'd, maples of various hues,
Scarlet and gold, and delicate streaks of pink
And purple blotches curiously wrought,
Inwoven with rich orange traceries
And dash'd with carmine, take the wandering eye
With ravishment, and dazzle at each glance :—
All quiet, in the calm of noon that now
Scarce floats the thistle's down, or stirs the leaf
Of tallest aspen on its poising stem,—
But toss'd against the blue-wall'd heavens, anon
And streaming in the fitful breezes, like
Banners and bannerets tumultuous borne
In conflict o'er the deadly battle-field!

        Out in the woods of Autumn! I have cast
Aside the shackles of the town, that vex
The fetterless soul, and come to hide myself,
Miami! in thy venerable shades.
Here where seclusion looks out on a scene
Of matchless beauty, I will pause awhile,
And on this bank with varied mosses crown'd
Gently recline. The forest has a voice

That comes to me with memories of her
Who bore me; and the beauty of the scene
Brings recollections up of some who here
Roam'd with me in my boyhood, who now walk
The ways of life no more: a thousand thoughts
Press on me, mingled with regretful pangs
For slight unkindnesses, not thought of then,
That now reproach me. What has been, thus haunts
What is. I feel the present and the past
Around me and within me. Earth is old,
And new; and so the heart, which is my world.

    Far in the quiet woodland! The calm sky
Looks smilingly upon me, and the air
Comes laden with the sweets of autumn time,
And living with the murmurs of the bee,
And insect tribes. Around me on the slopes
The aster blooms, and in the valley waves
The golden-rod. Beneath me, silver-bright,
Glide the calm waters, with a plaintive moan
For summer's parting glories. High o'erhead,
Seeking the sedgy brinks of still lagoons
That bask in southern suns the winter through,
Sails tireless the unerring waterfowl,
Screaming among the cloud-racks. Oft from where,
In bushy covert hid, the partridge stands,

  2

Bursts suddenly the whistle clear and loud,
Far-echoing through the dim wood's fretted aisles.
Deep murmurs from the trees, bending with brown
And ripened mast, are interrupted oft
By sounds of dropping nuts; and warily
The turkey from the thicket comes, and swift
As flies an arrow darts the pheasant down,
To batten on the autumn; and the air,
At times, is darkened by a sudden rush
Of myriad wings, as the wild pigeon leads
His squadrons to the banquet.   Far away,
Where tranquil groves on sunny slopes supply
Their liberal store of fruits, the merry laugh
Of children, and the truant school-boy's shout,
Ring on the air, as, from the hollows borne,
Nuts load their creaking carts, and lush pawpaws
Their motley baskets fill, with clustering grapes
And golden-sphered parsimmons spread o'er all.

Deep in the solemn forest !   From the tops
Of these old trees, swept by the evening wind,
Which swells among their leaves, and dies away,
And gathers strength again, float softly down
Strange, wild, deep harmonies.   And I have been
All day among the Voices of the Wood,
That are but echoes of perpetual tones
With which God fills the universe.   The noon,

Gairish and still, and midnight's calm repose,
And dewy eve, and fresh, rejoicing morn,
Are full of them.   I hear them in the breeze
That stirs the reed to music: in the faint,
Sad murmur of the stream that glides below,
Bearing away the fallen leaves, as pass
The dreams of childhood and the hopes of life,
I hear them: and I hear them in the spring
That, bubbling from beneath yon moss-clad root,
Falls tinkling o'er the shimmering rock below:
And in the billowy chimes that wake aloft
When freshening winds sweep through the ancient trees,
They speak with organ-tones, that reach the depths
Stirring within me, and an echo find
In the roused soul. . . .   O God! Thou art in all
I now behold! the essence and the life,
The germ and the vitality! the birth,
The being, and the end! else Reason gropes
In darkness all her days, and knowledge dies.
What but the high intelligence, the hand
Almighty, and the sempiternal life—
What but the omnipresence, and the will,
All which we feel thou art, and all that fills
Our great Idea of a primal cause,
And fix'd design beyond the power of chance
To change or check, could speak this glorious world
From wildest Chaos and profoundest Night?

What poise the planets in the void, and set
The infinite stars in order, and confine
Each in its separate path on high?   What fill
Earth with its countless forms of Life, and raise
Eternally, as ages glide along,
New being from the ashes of decay?

     Alone, with God and Nature, and this child
In whom I witness both.—Around me now
Is pressing onward the unceasing change.
And here, amid the thick-strewn vestiges
Of many centuries, whose paths are seen
Where time has worn these hollows in the hills,
And after beautified the ruin wrought
With all this growth of interlacing trees,
I contemplate the mysteries sublime
Of birth, and life, and death! . . From the dark womb
Of winter comes the spring with mild, warm breath;
And instantly the chains that bound the streams
Are loosened, and the waters leap to light,
And shout with gladness.   Soon the spell that long
Has held the earth, is broken; and the grass
Pierces the sod, and from the sheltering leaves
That strew the ground, look out the fresh young flowers,
Smiling to heaven.   Then the gray, leafless trees,
Long desolate in their utter nakedness,
Feel the new presence; and although no sign

Of life is visible, a delicate green
Creeps out along the tender twigs, where swell
The germ-infolding buds, and in the warm
And sunny day, and through the breezy night,
Come forth the myriad leaves, courting the light
And wantoning with the zephyr, till a robe
Of brightest green bursts on the wondering eye.
O'er the cold bosom of the sluggish clod
Soon steals the influence; and from the broad
And seeded field shoots up the waving grain,
Till spreads a sea of verdure far around,
Toss'd by the winds, and with the clouds at play.
Then comes the long and sunny summer time,
And for the garners of the husbandman
Ripens, and to the sickle lays, the grain;
And for the cherish'd tribes of air, that make
The cool groves vocal, strews the briary slope
With berries; and for the innumerous flocks
That shun the haunts of men, and hang their nests
High in the endless wood, or in the low
Dark thicket build, matures the beechen mast;
And takes the worm upon the leaf, and wraps
A silken tissue round it; and prepares
For many an insect race befitting tombs,
Where each shall sleep the winter hours away.
Then comes the lone and quiet autumn on,
With tinkling waterfalls, and moaning woods,

And arid wastes o'er which the night winds sigh.
And this is here; and now the flower hath closed
And cast its petals, and the naked stalk
Stands shriveling in the frost; the feathered grass
Is heavy in the head; the painted leaf
Flies twittering on the wind; and to the earth
Falls the brown nut, with melancholy sound.
Yet the low, moaning autumn wind, that sweeps
The seeded grass and lately-blossoming flower,
Bears the light germs of future life away,
And sows them by the gliding rivulet,
And o'er the plain, and on the mountain-side,
To clothe anew the earth, when comes again
The quickening breath of spring. And on the place
Where fall the ripened nuts, the frosty night
Will heap the stricken leaves; and thence shall spring,
In many an after age, another growth
Of stately trees, when those around me now,
Fallen with eld, shall moulder, and enrich
The ground that now sustains their lofty pride.

     Changing, forever changing!—So depart
The glories of the old, majestic wood;
So pass the pride and garniture of fields,
The growth of ages, and the bloom of days,
Into the dust of centuries; and so
Are both renewed. The scattered tribes of men,

The generations of the populous earth,
All have their seasons too.   And jocund Youth
Is the green springtime—Manhood's lusty strength
Is the maturing summer—hoary Age
Types well the autumn of the year—and Death
Is the real winter, which forecloses all.
—And shall the forests have another spring,
And shall the fields another garland wear,
And shall the worm come forth renewed in life
And clothed upon with beauty, and not man?
No!—in the Book before me now, I read
Another language; and my faith is sure,
That though the chains of death may hold it long,
This mortal will o'ermaster them, and break
Away, and put on immortality.

Almighty Father! such the lesson is,
That, in these cool and venerable woods,
Amid the relics of a mighty Past,
From which look out the strong and swelling germs
Of a still mightier Future,—Father, such
Is the great lesson that I read to-day,
With love and awe; and firmer in my breast,
By every syllable, these truths are fixed:
That Thou art the beginning, and the end,
Of all this wondrous work; and that Thy love
Pervades the universe; and that Thy smile

Seeketh all hearts to sun them; and that Thou
In every glorious thing we here behold,
Declarest and reveal'st Thyself to be
The Majesty Supreme—Eternal God.

Part Second.

1844.

AFTER long-wandering in the crowded streets
Of busy cities, where Humanity
Is least and greatest; after gay saloons,
And soft, seductive luxuries, and forms
Languidly beautiful, and oft-heard tones
Have pall'd upon the senses; what delight
Steals o'er the spirit, in the beautiful haunts
Of Nature, 'mid the silence, and the shade,
And low, sweet murmurs from the earth and air,
And all the holy influences that come
With blessèd gleams of the blue heavens above!

Society grows stale, and men become
Not what they were, or seemed to be.   We change—
All change, both to each other, and ourselves.
Our habitudes, our passions, our delights,
Are ever mutable.   But in these shades,
Amid these venerable trees, beneath
Yon blue o'erarching canopy, where'er
The unshorn majesty of Nature reigns,

3

There is a glorious, an abounding joy,
Forever. Not to haunts like these belong
The pallid cheek, the sickly frame, the roll
Of feelings grown untimely old:—But you,
Ye wild and wooded hills, ye flowery dales
That stretch between and bask in light, ye rocks
O'er which the cool springs trickle, and ye clear
And flashing rivulets, that run along
And murmur to the winds, which murmur back,
—Audible voices of the Deity!
—Visible impress of Almighty Power!
—Bright, bland expression of Creative Love!
Ye still are new and beautiful: and still
Within your calm and unpolluted depths
The thoughts are fresh, the springy limb doth long
Retain its elasticity, the heart
Broods not and sickens not o'er ills that fast
Beget each other, and the feelings know
An almost perpetuity of youth.

Far-seated in these mighty groves, I hear
The solemn Anthem of the Centuries
Roll up, as if the Majesty of God
Swept o'er the Universe, and spoke: the low,
Deep plaint of millions that have lived, and toil'd,
And died, in bondage—the despairing cry
Of struggling hearts that pour'd their torrents out,
And sank exhausted down beneath the hard

And crushing heel of tyranny—the sweet,
Sad interludes of mercy, and of love—
The glad songs of deliverance—the thick
And smothered voice of hate—the taunt of scorn—
The terrible threat of vengeance—the intense
Though whispered oaths that league determined men,
And know no revocation—and, o'er all,
The exulting shout of Freedom from the hills,
And from the plains, and from the empurpled seas!

And then peals out from billowy chimes of thought,
A wild, irregular song, that has such tune
As the sea sings with, and a symphony
Like unto that which gales from Labrador
Pipe in the shrouds when waves roll mountain high.

1.

Lift up your hearts, oh men!
From the long sorrow that has weigh'd them down:
Eternal Justice, from her starry height,
Stoops earthward through the dusk of centuries,
To poise anew the balance that shall weigh
Henceforth the relative rights
Of master and of man,
Of ten and of ten thousand, here on earth.
Lift up your weary hearts!—
Rejoice! rejoice!
Weighed in the scales, Oppression kicks the beam.

2.

Wrong liveth not for aye!
'T is not immortal, as is common Right:
Right and the Truth exist eternally,
But Wrong and Falsehood perish day by day;
They perish by their own inherent ill—
    While Truth, with brow serene,
    Lives in immortal bloom;
And Right, though baffled oft, in many ways,
    Rises and reigns at last.—
        Rejoice! rejoice!
Wrong cometh to its fall, as God is good.

3.

Lift up your hearts, oh men!
Stretch forth the arm, and try its unused strength;
Plant the foot firmly on the galling chain;
Brace every sinew to its utmost power;
Now with invincible will each muscle clothe:—
    Ha! how the fetters fall!
    Was this—was *this* a slave?
It looks so like a MAN, 't is hard to think
    It other than a man!—
        Rejoice! rejoice!
The Man ascends: the King comes to the dust.

A wild, hoarse song, but truthful.—As from out
The laboring bosom of the Carib Sea,
Isle after isle has sprung, rooted in rock
And ribb'd with adamant, which even now
Are to each other reaching out strong arms,
That yet shall clasp, and firmly interlace,
And circle into states confederate,
The beauty and the wonder of the world:
So, from the great profound of Thought, comes up
Truth after truth, compact and luminous,
Which, each with each uniting, intertwine,
Till, girt with principle and grooved in right,
Broad systems form that are the strength of man
And bulwarks of his freedom.—We behold
Cycle and epicycle rounding back
Into infinitude.   We cannot see
The end from the beginning.   Only this
With something like assurance stamps itself
Upon the mind: that the great cycle of all,
In which these cycles move, starts from the base
In an ascending grade that knows no check,
Runs circle after circle, never joined,
And strengthens to the summit.   This supplies
Larger and larger fields for man, and gives
The soul that larger freedom which it seeks,
And has sought from the first, continually:
And with the larger freedom, still must come

The larger forms it covets, and with these
The full enfranchisement of man, which is
The aim and the attainment of the Soul:
For full enfranchisement is faith, and love,
And charity, and peace o'er all the earth.
    Hope is from Heaven: then let man not despair!
The Plan of the Eternal moves right on:
It knows no ebb—it makes no pause—it has
No Ajalon. The cycles fill the void,
In the great Cycle upward moving still,
And resting in Perfection, full-attained
Here and Hereafter—not in either state
Alone, but in both only.—Men despair,
Sicken and die, believing that the base,
Unscrupulous arts by which their fellow men
O'erreach each other, must destroy the poise
Of Right forever, and to chaos back
Hurl frail Humanity. But God's high scheme
Depends not on contingencies like these:
Men, the poor instruments, may fail in faith
Among themselves, and lack fidelity
To truth, to justice, mercy, love, and all
That human reason deems essential: yet,
God overrules each wrong for right, and still
The great design moves on and on, while all
Who falter, perish in their faithlessness.

This is the lesson Meditation reads,
Sitting in solitude on mossy rocks,
Or walking hand in hand with Nature, here
In her great temples, arch'd with heaven's own blue,
And pillared with the majesty of trees
That have the strength of centuries.—To one
Who in these quiet halls is far removed
From human passions, vain desires, the throes
Of party, and the conflicts of the field,
How paltry, wicked, miserable, mean,
Seem the contentions of society!

Turn, thou whose ears have drunk the jarring
        sounds
Of wrangling tongues, in crowded thoroughfares
And busy marts—or thou whose eyes have looked
On the red battle-field, and there beheld
The quivering limb, the writhing countenance,
The blackened and the putrifying corpse—
Turn from all this, which liker is to hell
Than to aught else, and with thy soul commune,
Here in the quiet of Miami Woods.
—Look out upon the bordering fields, where spreads
The yellow wheat, and waves the tasseling corn;
Look in, where the great heart of Nature beats
Steadily, peacefully, ever full of love;
Look down, at the sweet flowers that clothe the ground,

Blooming for all, and giving thankfully
Their perfume for the light that visits them;
Look up, at the blue heavens that bend o'er all,
Serene, and beautiful, and grand, and good :
Then, if thou wonderest, ask this little child,
Whose soul is awed to silence, what there is
In all this scene, that *thou* should'st thus be call'd
From the great world where beats the human heart
In all its power, and she will answer—" GOD,
And God's own peace, and majesty, and strength!"
—In such a Presence, bend thy stubborn neck,
And stand uncovered. God, not man, is here;
Nature, not art; dissimulation not,
But frankness; falsehood never, only truth.
And if thou go not hence a better man,
Pray fervently for help—for thou hast need.

Sage monitors of youth are wont to say
The eye grows early dim to nature's charms,
And commerce with the world soon dulls the ear
To heavenliest sounds. It may be so; but I,
Whose feet were on the hills from earliest life,
And in the vales, and by the flashing brooks,
Have not so found it :—deeper in my heart,
Deeper and deeper year by year, has sunk
The love of nature, in my close, and long,
And fond companionship with woods and waves,

With birds and breezes, with the starry sky,
The mountain-height, the rocky gorge, the slope
Mantled with flow'rs, and the far-reaching plain
That mingles with the heavens.   It is not so—
It is not so save where the ear grows dull
To God's own voice, and the averted eye,
Thick film'd with sin, is darkened thus, and lost
To all his visible glory.   The green fields
Are studded with their golden buttons still,
And living with their gilded butterflies,
That pass not unobserved.   The rocky pool,
In which the robin bathes his dusky plumes,
The tufted flow'rs that smile beyond, the slope
That from its margin greenly steals away
To bordering woodlands fill'd with airy tongues,
Still lure us from the hot and dusty road
As in the years gone by.   There come at morn,
From the cool groves and from the orchards round,
The same sweet songs of birds that charm'd the ear
Of childhood, and of youth ; and in the eve
Floats up from the broad meadows still, the same
Sweet smell of new-made hay.   Day and the Sun
In all his glory—Night and all she hath
Of beauty, or of mystery, or joy,
Still hold their spell upon the heart, and fill
The soul with wonder and with awe.   The earth
Fades not, and fails not in its wealth of charms :—

We seek them now, as in our earliest years,
And find them: we plunge far into the woods,
And roam the flowery fields, and climb the hills,
Not less the child that we are more the man:
We loiter where the waters of the brook
Dance down the pebbly slope, and watch the leaf
Or feather that is on its bosom borne,
Till lost to sight: the little hand that scoop'd
The cool wave up in childhood, larger grown,
Needs now no prompting, but supplies the draught
To thirsty lip or heated forehead.   Now,
As then, we marvel at the growing grass,
And at the blooming flower, and at the tree
That rises up and pierces the blue sky
Among the clouds.   The high heav'n-spanning arch,
That evening builds when storm has roll'd away
And dies far east, the purple sunset's hue,
The unmatch'd iris of the humming-bird,
The rose's cup, the lily's silver bell,
The blue-eyed violet—*all* sights and sounds
That won the eye or charm'd the ear in youth,
Are living still.   Eternal beauty dies
Within man's heart but through eternal sin,
Or with annihilation.   He who has
The love of right, the fear of wrong, the hate
And scorn of evil, multiform and dark—
Who hearkens to the still small voice within—

Who hourly bids the hourly tempter back—
Who loves his fellow-men—who leaves to Heav'n
The judgment of his enemies: not to him,
Not to his eye, not to his ear, will God
Willingly suffer the glad sights and sounds
Of nature to grow dim, or to become
Inaudible.   *Years* change us not so much,
Nor commerce with the world; but groveling thoughts,
Vaulting ambitions, unrepressed desires,
Whose oft-indulgence blunts the edge of youth:
These early dim the eye to nature's charms,
And early dull the ear to heavenliest sounds.

My thoughts, exultant o'er the strides of time,
Flow as they list in novel cadences.—
A cheerful melody, learned long ago,
But half forgotten now, comes stealing up
Among remembered tones of other years,
And breaks in fitful murmurs from my lips:—
To this the currents of my musing flow

1.

How lightly on yon wave the wild duck sits,
Now floating with the current, and anon
Eddying the drowsy hours of noon away
    Where minnows sport, and where
    The lushest sedges grow!—
So lightly sits the youth upon my heart.

2.

How brightly yet, down this sequestered dell,
Lie the cool drops of rain that fell last night,
In the leaf's hollow and the wildflower's cup,
    Though the hot, scorching sun,
    Has been for hours athirst!—
So brightly lies the youth upon my heart.

3.

How fondly unto yon high tree, that lifts
Its folds from chilling shadows to the sun,
And there supports them when the tempests rage,
    Clings the dependent vine,
    By every tendril clings!—
So fondly clings the youth unto my heart.

4.

How sweetly on this knoll the sunshine rests,
Filling with joy the moss's wondrous cup,
And calling violets, bluer than the sky,
    From their long winter sleep,
    To bless the earth again!—
So sweetly rests the youth upon my heart.

5.

How freshly lies, within the sweet embrace
Of these encircling hills, whose flowery slopes

Stretch to its marge, this clear and shining pool,
    Whose waters ever flow
    From yon half hidden rock!—
So freshly lies the youth within my heart.

    A simple melody, got long ago:
A cheerful thought, more difficult to learn.—
So lightly, fondly, sweetly, freshly lies
The youth within my heart: so rest it there!
'Tis only feeling makes us old: our years
But bear us toward the grave. We all must die,
But must not all grow old, except in years.
—The groves, whose beauty and whose music stole
Into my wondering spirit long ago,
Were ne'er more beautiful than now, were ne'er
More musical. I come and walk the ways
Of boyhood, and I find the flowers the same:
I pause, and sit in old familiar seats,
And see no change, save that the gathering mold
Is greener, and that now upon them press
Mosses and lichens of a few more years.—
The youth is in the heart of Nature, too!

    Beautiful, beautiful Youth!—Freshness is youth,
And truthfulness is youth, and innocence;
And faith, and love, and joyousness are youth:
Whatever undistorted stands, and wears

The impress and the glow with which at first
It came from God, is panoplied in youth.
It gathers not the dust of time—it takes
No tarnish from the earth—but walks abroad
Effulgent with the glory of its Source,
And trailing robes of beauty evermore.

My soul is full; and from its stirring depths,
Oh, beautiful young heart! whose tendrils cling
So closely round my own, flow, overflow,
These fervent strains to thine:—

1.

Child of my love!
Count it a blessing that thou also art
The child of Nature, and the lineal heir
Of all the wealth of charms that she bestows
Upon her votaries

2.

The morning air,
That to thy chamber, ere thou art awake,
Comes with cool lips, fresh-bathed in meadowy dews,
And kisses thy young cheek; the choral songs,
That on the freshening breeze, from ringing groves,
Float sweetly up and sing thee from thy sleep;
The glittering grass, that in the sun's first beam

Mimics the midnight heav'ns; the holy calm
That, like a blessed influence from God,
Prompts thy young heart to prayer: these, loved one,
    these
        Are of thy heritage.

3.

        The solemn hush
Of summer noons,—when o'er the city sweeps,
Sirocco-like, each fitful breath of air,
Till men sink down exhausted, and for hours,
In languid half-repose, fond mothers lie
And fan their suffering infants,—comes to thee
With cheerful gleams of blue and peaceful skies,
And quiet whispers from sweet pebbly brooks,
That glide along in shadow, mingled oft
With drowsy murmurs, in the sunny air,
Of many insect tribes, and fitful songs
From dark ancestral cedars stealing out,
Where wearied wings are folded. Blessed lot!
Which thou inheritest, and dost possess,
        As Nature's child and mine.

4.

        Thine is the eve
Of healthful breezes that come freshening up
From springy dells and wooded wild ravines,

From broad, clear rivers, where they've kiss'd the wave
And stolen its coolness, and from pastoral slopes
Alive with herds, whose breath they've gathered up
In all its sweetness, and now bring to thee.
The oriole greets thee from his hanging bower;
The sparrow sings for thee; the southern wren
Echoes the cardinal's resounding notes;
The catbird leads the Vespers sweetly on,
Till sets the sun; and then the hermit thrush,
Quiet all day in far-off thickets, comes
Nearer at night's approach, and pours his soul
In ravishing melodies, till all the air
    Is living with his spirit.

5.

    And thine the night,
All starr'd with glory, and all fill'd with tones
That come down from the Infinite, and link
Our being with the elder-born of Time,
Eternity, Existence uncreate:
Voices that speak in dreams, or memories,
Or consciousness yet faint and undefined,
Of Pre-existence—states, conditions, forms,
That are not now, but whither we are borne,
To the Inevitable and the Doom,
May be again, or not, as now and here
    We haply win or lose.

6.

    Child of my love!
Oh, count it fortunate thou art the child
Of Nature also.   To this double bond
Be faithful.   Coming years will tempt thee sore—
But in the trials and the triumphs Life
May have in store for thee, forget thou not
The haunts wherein thy childhood met with love,
And peace, and beauty; where in tranquil ways
Thy chafing spirit thou didst often soothe;
And where, as thy young heart has felt, God walked
    With Nature and with thee.

Part Third.

1851.

The spring is here, an ever-welcome joy,
With all its gifts of leaf, and bud, and flower,
And all its wealth of breeze, and bird, and song:
And I am with the spring—a sharer free
In all the sweet delights she brings from heaven,
And scatters o'er the earth with liberal hand.

How grateful are these haunts, up into which
I now ascend, to one whose spirit chafes
Amid the din of cities, where so much
That is the work of human hands appears,
And where remains so little that was God's!
Above me, patches of blue sky are shown;
Below, mosaic-plats reach far away,
Of varied mosses made, and shining grass,
And early flowers, lit up by quivering flakes
Of sun that, struggling through the swaying trees,
Fall warm to earth; while scattered all around,
Where openings give the breeze and sun free play,
Are sweet-briar clumps, and natural arbors made
By wild-grapes clambering over dogwood tops,

And trailing thence to earth.   About my brow,
Drying the locks which the long winding walk
Has moistened, freshly play soft meadowy winds,
That bear the violet's breath from sunny nooks,
And from the blossoms of the pendant vine
Steal odors sweeter than the spicy airs
Of Eden, that revisit us in dreams.
Clear, purling rills, that lave the calamus-root,
And gently glide among the mint and cress,
Then dance and sparkle where the pebbly bed
Slopes to the brimming pool, sing o'er again
The songs of Siloa's brook, erst heard of old
By prophets in the groves of Palestine.
Nor wind and wave alone; but all the wide
Green wood is voiceful; and from fretted roof,
And groined arch, rolls out an anthem sound,
Whose clear, deep tones, make these primeval halls,
Spreading in many-pillared majesty,
Holy and beautiful. .   .   .   .   Eternal God!
Thanks for the freshness of the early spring!
Thanks for the flowers in unfrequented ways
That bud and bloom! and for the feathered tribes
Which dart like arrows by, and fill the groves
With melody! and for the towering trees
That wall this temple in, 'not made with hands,'
In which I worship! Thanks, Supremest Good,
For the soft airs that blow upon me now!

And for the sunny hills and grassy plains
O'er which they wander, like the murmuring bee,
Gathering all subtle essences at will!
And for all sights, and sounds, and perfumes sweet,
That make the ecstasy which here I feel,
Accept these thanks, O Father. . . . I am here,
Again, MIAMI! mid the holy calm
That in the soul of thy vast solitude
Reigns ever, save when broken by the rush
Of tempests, or the harsh and terrible tones
Of thunder, that with arrowy lightnings come
And pierce thy still recesses. I am here—
The same, yet not the same, as when at first,
In mild, reflective mood, and artless verse,
I sang thy charms, and lifted from their midst
My heart to God. The same, yet not the same:
For on the dial-plate of Life, since then,
The shadow of my quickly rounding years
Has numbered twelve. And I have wandered far,
And much have seen of glory and of grief;
And much have known of pleasure and of pain;
And much have thought of human pride and pomp,
Which are the sorriest and baldest things
The indulgent eye of Heaven looks down upon.
The same, yet not the same: three cherub forms
Have lain within my partner's breast, since then,
That now lie in the earth—three birdlings fair

Sung on my knee, that sing in heaven now.
And one who oftenest wandered with me here,
The wildest and the merriest that then
Had blessed our love and hope, in whom I saw
Renewed the freshness of my youth, and felt
Again its mantling bloom, in darkness now
And dreariness is whelm'd, by sad eclipse
Of reason, and attending woes that wear
The body thin, and vex the spirit.   Here,
Haply, she may not come again; but here,
In her bright youth and all-abounding love,
She'll live with me forever, though the gloom
That wraps her now mysterious Providence
May ne'er dispel.   The same, yet not the same:
'T was Autumn then in thy deep heart, which mourn'd
Its summer glories, passing fast away;
But in my own, perpetual fountains played,
And to perpetual hopes, that clustered there,
Gave brightest bloom.   But Autumn now has come
To *my* bereavèd heart, which inly moans
For withered hopes and blighted flowers of love,
While thine is full of gushing melodies,
And sunniest slopes, and green and bloomy nooks.

Sorrow is not despair, but rather hope :—
And thus again my pensive musings flow
To snatches of another melody,

That in the heat of feeling now come out
On the dim plain of memory, as stamps
Worn and obliterated long from coin,
By fire are to the surface brought again.

1.

    Ah! well-a-way!
The cloud will come; but after comes the sun.
Youth lies within the heart, and youth and sorrow
Were never strangers since the Eden-fall.
Sorrow descends upon the flower of youth,
As snow upon the crimson April-bloom,
Not with a blighting chill, but with a soft
And kindly pressure, that to youth gives strength,
Warmth to the crimson blossom, and to both
    The panoply that shields
    From after-coming storms.

2.

    Ah! well-a-way!
Sin was begot in Hell, and sorrow born
In Eden, but the two are ever twinn'd.
Without the sin the sorrow might not come:
But with the sin, the sorrow is a bright,
Redeeming angel, pointing to a time
When sin was not; to an eternity
When sin shall be no more; and to a God

Who in his mercy gave the sorrow birth,
  That thus the sin might die,
  And man again be pure.

  So sang I but a little month ago,
Walking within ambrosial groves, that look'd
Out on green pastures, over gleaming waves.
And now, so quickly in this genial clime
The fair and fruitful seasons follow on,
The bright and full-robed summer-time is here.
—How beautifully glimmer on my sight
The fresh green fields afar!   How grandly rise
The groves that gloom around me!   What a hush
Broods o'er this dell!   And how yon hillside basks
In the full blaze of this unspotted day!
All these have been my haunts from childhood up;
And only recent years have made my feet
Once unfamiliar with their flowery paths.
But absence has not robbed them of a charm,
Nor distance of their sweet attractiveness;
And my heart turns to them as to old friends.

  Morn after morn my footsteps hither tend;
Noon after noon the slumberous silence fills
My yearning heart, which still has aching voids;
Eve after eve I linger here alone,
Piercing the shadow of the day that is,

To find the sunlight of the days that were.
—The April flush has parted from the woods;
The redolent airs of May have gone to rest
With locust-tassels and the wild-grape's bloom;
The blue-eyed violet no more is seen
Peeping from mossy coverts at the sky
That looks down through the tree-tops; from the slopes
The tremulous anemone is gone;
The dandelions, that on the grassy plains
Were beautiful,—flecks from the golden curls
Of bright Aurora thrown,—have pass'd away.
These were the firstlings of the opening Year;
And like the firstlings of the human heart,
The beautiful young hopes that spring to light
And perish as the sterner days come on,
They are no more. A statelier growth is now
Giving green glory to the forest-aisles,
And beauty to the meadows. Far away
The alder-thicket, robed in brightest bloom,
Is shining like a sunlit cloud at rest;
Nearer, the briar-roses load the air
With sweetness; and where yon half-hidden fence
And toppling cabin mark the Pioneer's
First habitation in the wilderness,
The gay bignonia to the ridge-pole climbs,
The yellow willow spreads its generous shade
Around the cool spring's margin, and the old

And bent catalpa waves its fan-like leaves
And lifts its milk-white blossoms.   Beautiful!
Around me here rise up majestic trees
That centuries have nurtured: graceful elms,
Which interlock their limbs among the clouds;
Dark-columned walnuts, from whose liberal store
The nut-brown Indian maids their baskets fill'd
Ere the first Pilgrims knelt on Plymouth Rock;
Gigantic sycamores, whose mighty arms
Sheltered the Redman in his wigwam prone,
What time the Norsemen roamed our chartless seas;
And towering oaks, that from the subject plain
Sprang when the builders of the tumuli
First disappeared, and to the conquering hordes
Left these, the dim traditions of their race
That rise around, in many a form of earth
Tracing the plain, but shrouded in the gloom
Of dark, impenetrable shades, that fall
From the far centuries.   Eternal night,
Rayless and ruthless, where this luminous day
Displays its varied and resplendent charms!
I turn from that to these, as from a book
Whose lids are sealed, to one whose open leaves
Are full of wisdom and of beauty.   See!
How through the high-arch'd windows of the trees
That line this bank, the fresh green landscape glows!
And how from the broad mirror of yon stream

The glinting rays of the bright sun are turn'd!
Like fiery arrows quivering through the gloom
Of forest-aisles, they glance upon me now,
But break in golden fragments round my feet.

The quiet of a tranquil mind is where
Yon homestead stands amid embowering vines,
And clustering fruits; and where yon merry groups
Of children sit beneath the maple shade,
Wreathing sweet garlands for each other's bright
And sunny brows, is innocence; and where
Yon plowman meditates amidst his corn,
Dark and luxuriant, Plenty sits and smiles!
And Peace is heard, in many a gentle sound
Of tinkling bell and lowing cattle, where
Yon herd knee-deep in lushest grasses feeds,
And where yon mower from his heavy swath
Rises, and rests, and whets his ringing scythe.
On the green, skirting slope that lies beyond,
Where fitful shadows with the sunshine play,
And where white flocks in statue-like repose
Are gathered under solitary elms,
There sleeps the beauty of a dream of Heaven.
And over all the scene the calm blue sky
Bends in its summer glory, stooping down
Amid soft clouds that kiss the sunny cheeks
Of airy hills, and there hang motionless.

How beautiful! how joyous! how serene!
Yet oh! how desolate, bereft of her
Into whose young and all-impressive heart
The silence and the beauty of the scene
So deeply sank when first she hither came.
Her years then numbered ten; and six since then
Have woven their summer garlands for her brow;
And one has brought the cypress and the yew,
And laid upon her heart—her glad young heart!
The day was one, like this, of untold charms.
Earth, heaven, the waters, and the wandering winds,
Each lent its tribute to make up a whole
Whose memories are written, even now,
In lines of light which darkness can not dim.
We wandered up and down; now in these groves,
Now on the rims of meadow-plats, anon
Far in the silent wood.   A summer's day
She gathered flowers, and mock'd the birds, and blew
The time o' the day on grey-beard dandelions.
When eve approached, we hither came, and paused,
Struck with the various beauty of the scene.
She sat beside me on this grassy knoll,
That looks out on it all, and gazed and gazed
Until that mind, so darken'd now, was fill'd
With light from heaven, and love for earth, and joy
That in such pleasant places God had cast
Our lot.   We lingered till the sun went down;

Then, silent as the shadows of the night
That gathered round us, took our homeward way.

    Sweet scene! sweet memories! how ye brighten up,
And throng the ways that to the burdened heart
Lead in, with incidents of many years
Crowding a single moment! . . . Time wore on:
Her school—my avocations—city life,
That puts so many fetters on the limbs,
Conspired to limit, and at times prevent.
Our visits to the farther solitudes,
And green savannas, and cool, vocal groves,
That in the bosom of Miami Woods
Still offer to the over-wearied heart
The silence and the solace that it craves.
But nothing made us strangers *here:*—we came
When came the bluebird and the violet—
And when the summers put their glory on,
We stood within its radiance—and our hearts
Grew pensive in the golden quietude
That came when Autumn brought her misty airs,
And sang the season's requiem. Not a year,
Of five that flow'd in light and beauty on,
Pass'd over without bringing us to bathe
Our spirits in the quiet pools of Thought
That lay unruffled here. Her early love
Of Nature, fostered by these interviews,

Grew stronger day by day, and through the bonds
Of common sympathy, she soon became
A part of all this scene, and it of her.
I see her now, through shadows and through tears,
In all her beauty wandering by my side,
And hear her voice, with snatches of old song,
Swell up, and die away, and wake again.
—Vain apparition! memories vainer still!
Ye make me feel how much alone I am,
More than I felt before: ye bend the bow,
And barb the arrows that transfix my heart.

Oh, from this scene the bloom hath faded now;
And that which was the soul of it to me,
The glory and the grace, sits far away,   .
Beneath the shadow of a sorrow big
With all that can affright, or overwhelm.

. . . My heart would break—my stricken heart
        would break,
Could I not pour upon the murmuring winds,
When thus it swells, the burden of its woe,
In words that soothe, how sad soe'er they be.

1.

Sweet bird that, deep in beechen shades embower'd,
Sittest and pour'st the sorrow of thy heart,

Till all the woods around
Throb as in heavy grief—
Mourn now with me: in deepest shades of sorrow
Sits my lone heart, and pours its plaint of woe,
Till in sad unison
Throbs every heart around.

2.

Sweet brook, that over shining pebbles glidest
In quiet, with a low and plaintive moan,
Made to the listening woods
And to the leaning flowers—
Mourn now with me: like thine my life in quiet
Glides on and on, with songs of flowers and woods;
Nor asks a gayer scene,
Or other auditors.

3.

Sweet summer wind, that, high among the branches
Of elm, and poplar, and of towering oak,
Sighest the morning out,
Sighest the evening in—
Mourn now with me: in and from early boyhood,
I've loved with you these lone and sinless haunts,
Nor asked to pour my song
Where the proud world might hear.

4.

Sweet bird, sweet brook, sweet summer wind, oh listen!
Come to me from the throbbing beechen shade,
From moaning hollows come,
And from the sighing trees—
Mourn now with me: mourn for the dear one absent,
Who loved you with a love as strong as mine:
Mourn for the mind's eclipse—
Unutterable woe!

Beyond the cloud that darkens the sweet morn
The sun shines ever. When the rain has pass'd,
The grass is robed in diamonds, and the pools
Dimple with every breeze. Behind the tears
That gather in the gentle maiden's eyes
When feelingly she sings her saddest song,
The laugh lurks ever, showing bright through all,
And bringing to her bosom quick relief.
Sorrow is strong; and from its roots, that clasp
Rebellious passions in the Eden-life,
It sends out folds that wind about the heart,
And tendrils that cling to it evermore:
But these oft beautify, and even at times
Support; and were this never so, beyond
The roots of sorrow lies the birth of hope—
And hope is mightier than sorrow, far.

Part Fourth.

1852.

MIAMI WOODS! From busy scenes of life,
Of vaunting littleness and fretting state,
Of vain ambitions and repulsive pride,
Of sin, and sorrow, and nefarious wrong,
I come again for meditation, peace,
And healthful exercise, to these far haunts,
Where human passions have not yet destroy'd
The calm repose, the majesty, the might,
Of Nature. Summer here has garlanded
The pillars of these glorious temples round,
And laid the light mosaic floor, and built
The groinèd arches, and spread out above
The fretted roof. And here I gladly steal
From the hot glare of day, and from the strife
Of ever-clashing interests, that make
Society the thing it should not be,
Not only to commune with my own soul
In solitude, but 'mid these calm retreats
To contemplate the busy world without,
Its higher aims, its littleness, its pride,
And the gigantic meannesses that make

Sin of repute by contrast! . . . Come with me,
Ye whose hearts sicken at the tales of woe,
Oppression, avarice, hatred, lust and war,
Which faster than the winds now fly about:
Stand with me here upon the forest's edge,
And look out on the quiet, happy homes,
That dot the landscape, each with plenty bless'd,
And crown'd with sweet content, so rarely found:
See the broad, sunny fields of ripening grain,
How peacefully they lie! the orchards see,
Loaded with shining fruits! the garden spots,
Bright with their vegetation! and the wide,
Smooth meadow-lands, with lowing herds alive,
And bleating flocks! Look out upon it all—
Its peace, its plenty, its sequestered joys—
And say if *this* shall e'er become the scene
Of blood and carnage: if disastrous war, .
With rampant horrors and unsparing lust,
Shall ever desolate these happy homes!
—The plains of Greece, Italia's sunny vales,
All Europe's broad expanse, fit answer give,
If human passions rule without restraint,
And bold ambition be not held in check.

What is the lesson of the past? O'er earth,—
So runs the bloody chronicle,—the sword
Has claim'd dominion ever. By the plow

Patient and toiling industry has striven,
And turn'd the soil, and planted; but the sword
Has cut the harvest, and its myrmidons
Have filled their garners first.   To charge and hold
The distaff, and to ply the busy wheel,
Has been the woman's office; but the spear
Has caught the thread upon its gory point,
And had it woven into trappings gay
For conquering legions.   Where the falchion flash'd
The cross has crumbled: where the battle-shout
Has risen, there the prayer has died away:
And in the populous valleys, where the tramp
Of armèd hosts has sounded like the sea,
'Mid rapine, and debauch, and smoke, and flame,
The happy homes of innocence and peace
Have disappeared.   Ambition, leagued with lust,
Laid his red hand upon the ancient world,
And it stood still with terror.—Earth again,
In these the later years, has been the scene
Of deadliest conflicts, till terrific throes
Have rent the bosom of society.
Thrones then have rock'd, and rulers stood aghast,
As if this solid and substantial orb
Were quaking under them, and gaping seams
Hissed for their quick engulfment.   Wild, and fierce,
And desolating periods have pass'd,
Till Horror's maw was glutted, and he sank

Sated with blood.   Peace then has come again,
With her benignant voice, and countenance
Haloed like a divinity's; and men,
 Led captive by her many beautiful ways,
And by the majesty that girt her round,
And by the providence that she displayed,
And by the prosperous arts that sprung to life
Where'er she pass'd, have risen and followed her.

   But still the sword asserts dominion; still
War eateth out the substance of the lands:
And when, oh! when shall human tongue proclaim,
Peace is the throned divinity of Earth!
Order and Freedom are her ministers!

   Order and Freedom! this God's highest gift,
That his primordial law—distinct, yet one—
For without union neither can endure,
This running wild, that darting from the grooves
Of due adjustment.   How the equipoise
Fails in the roll of nations from the first!
That is not FREEDOM, which of old in Greece
Oiled the glib tongues of cunning orators,
Till with proclaimed respect for human rights
The walls of senates echoed that which was,
If not the hollowest mockery and scorn,
A blistering satire on the very name

Of Liberty.   That is not Freedom which
Has fed so oft Parisian guillotines
With blood that cried to God and man for quick
And terrible revenge.   Nor freedom that,
No matter who or what may call it so,
Which is, in any form, but foul misuse
Of liberty to think, and speak, and act:
'T is but licentiousness, and soon or late,
By boisterous and brutish courses, thwarts
The end it aims at.   Nor is ORDER that
Which reigned in Warsaw, when the red-winged scourge
From Russia madly swept o'er Poland's plains.
Nor Order that which gave to modern Rome
A seeming quiet, when the serried ranks
Pass'd from the bubbling chaos that is France,
And stilled the awakening soul of Right
And Freedom on the fields of old renown.
Order is never that, whate'er its name,
Which moves engirt by intellectual thralls,
Or bristling iron flashing stern command :
This is but chain'd disorder, that, with eyes
Which never sleep, and sinews ne'er unbraced,
Watches and waits its moment, when, self-loosed,
It breaks all bounds, and mocks all consequence—
Prostrating by its fierce, convulsive throes,
Order and freedom both : then Chaos reigns.

Dread picture—dark and dread! My Country, thou
Who sitt'st among the nations like a queen
On whom all eyes are fixed, upon thy brow
The Khoinoor of regal gems is worn—
The Mount of Light, within whose steady ray
The wandering feet of millions hither tend:
Oh, may the blight of faction, and the curse
Of dark cabal, be spared thy generous breast!
Thou art the hope of Freedom, and the dread
Of Tyranny.   Within thy bosom lies
A nursling giant, slumbering now, who thence
Shall draw the strength which fabling bards of old
Bestowed on world-sustaining Atlas.   Grant,
Oh, Thou who mak'st the courses of the stars,
And art no less the guide and guard of man,
That when this germ of mightiest power shall reach
Its certain and its due development,
It shall not smite, with matricidal hand,
The bosom that hath nourished it; but give
Its majesty of strength, its cumulate
Of wisdom, its capacity for good,
To Man, to Truth, to Freedom, and to God!

Time writes upon the earth, in many ways,
Wise admonition, that man's eagle eye,
Bent on the stars in cold ambition's heaven,
Stoops not to read.   The far-away, the dim,

The difficult, who sees not? 'T is the plain,
Whose lessons lie along our daily paths,
That none behold, or comprehend.   And yet,
The palpable is eloquent.   There lies
A column, where a Grecian temple stood:
There stands a crumbling wall where Roman might
Built up its proudest structure:—Both relate
The self-same story of aggressive power,
Of wild ambition for extended rule,
And of intestine strifes that live on blood,
And die in desolation.   Far away
From these dark relics and their lesson—far,
Where the adventurous Genoese descried
Another world, and gave it to the free,
There hangs a picture of gigantic size
And wonderful design.   Although, as yet,
In any part unfinished, and in some
Almost untouched, it still displays in all
A towering genius, and a master hand.
It shows a nearly limitless expanse
Of hill and vale, of mountain and of plain.
Wide-spreading forests strike the wildered eye,
At first, of gorgeous foliage, varied hue,
And most majestic height.   Savannas green
Between the mountain ranges stretch away,
Till in the endless wood they lose themselves,
Or mingle with the sky, and of its blue

Become an undistinguishable part.
Down the deep gorges of the mountain sides
Careering torrents tumble.   Runnels leap
In cataracts white as wool from rock to rock,
And plunge in dark abysses.   O'er the plains
Gigantic rivers hold their solemn way,
Now disappearing in the wilderness,
Now flashing back the light of sun and stars.
Far in the background of this wondrous scene,
Where matchless Power has stooped and hollowed out
Stupendous basins in the eternal rock,
Vast lakes repose in majesty, that have
No parallels on earth.   Minuter view,
Scanning the picture close in all its parts,
Discloses habitations on the slopes
Of gentle hills, and sunny intervales
Covered with grain, and orchards bending low
With rich and ripening fruits, and grassy fields
Where the cow fills her udder, and the lamb
Crops undisturbed.   And other scrutiny
Reveals the prosperous city here and there,
Wherein are practiced the fair arts of peace,
And virtue brings its crowning joy, content.
The prostrate column, and the crumbling wall,
That tell of desolation, are not here.
No footprints of the Past reveal themselves
O'er all this wide domain, save in the wrecks

Of an extinguished race that lie around—
The tomb, the altar and the citadel,
Which Time in his long lapse has robed in green
Softer than velvet, making beautiful
Not only what were desolation else,
But the wide prospect round. The pillar'd pride
Of lofty groves, the dark luxuriant growth
Of virgin plains, and the resistless sweep
Of rivers on whose marge the bison-herd
And antlered elk feed quietly, proclaim,
That for the footsteps of the Future, here
Lie the appointed ways. Above the lone
And prostrate column, Memory may weep,
And by the crumbling wall: but joyous Hope
Comes with high courage and elastic limb,
And to each mountain of this marvelous scene,
And to each valley, points and leads the way.

Ah! Hope is strong to nations—strong to me:
But the bright ray that broke upon my path
When last I wandered in these silent shades,
Soon blackened like the night around my heart:
For darkness dreader than its first eclipse
O'erwhelmed again that young and struggling mind,
Which here had opened first to gleams of Truth,
And brightened to the Beautiful around.

Miami Woods! from these sequestered haunts
For many a long and weary month, till now,
Again I've been an exile, sick at heart,
And brooding o'er the sorrow of my life—
A sorrow that has been baptized in tears
So often, it is holier grown than love,
Or hope, or memories that perish not.

Again I stand by the remembered shrines
At which she earliest worship'd God with me.
How strongly seems her youthful impress fixed
On every thing around!   E'en now my soul
Is busy with a faint and simple chime,
To which the waving leaf and murmuring breeze
Bear sweet accompaniment, in full accord.

1.

Cool summer woods!   I walk not now alone:
The form of her whose darkness makes my woe,
Childlike as when she last was with me here,
Gleams brightly on me from the undergrowth,
And glides anear me in the deepening shade,
    As if she were not far, ah! far away.

6

2.

Dim forest walks!   That young and radiant face
Looks out from every silent bush around,—
And that glad voice, which rang so often here,
Breaks ever and anon from flowery nooks
And sunny knolls that were her chief delight,
    As if she were not far, ah! far away.

3.

Sweet, calm retreats!   From old familiar paths,
From favorite seats beside the babbling spring,
From leafy coverts close along my way,
I see her start in many a graceful bound,
With wildwood garlands bright upon her brows,
    As if she were not far, ah! far away.

Sad, soothing chime—it lingers on the air
In sweet reverberations, like the sounds
Of far-off bells, that in the hush of night
Cease not, but pass into our dreams; and now,
The waving leaf and murmuring breeze prolong
Its closing cadence, till the creeping brook,
The tinkling water-fall, the drowsy eve,
Repeat the burden, echoing to my heart
In plaintive measures, " Far, ah! far away!"

Part Fifth.

1852.

CALM, still retreats, I visit you again :
Now with a face of gladness, and a heart
None the less swelling with its gratitude
Because despair was never quite despair.
God has been merciful ! Where darkness dwelt
The light has come again, and with its rays
The phantoms of the mind have vanished.   Hush
Even the whispering zephyrs, while I kneel
And breathe my invocation ! . . .   Come to me,
Ye birds that go not when the summer goes :
Pause in your winding way, ye murmuring streams :
Gather about me, ye soft autumn airs
That linger in the woodlands yet, and play
Above the sunny meadows : still look up,
Pale, perishing blossoms, from your dusky couch
Of fallen leaves : lean forward now, ye rocks,
And trees, and hills, that your dull ears may catch
The faintest accent of my trembling voice,
While fervently I thank the God of all
For this last mercy to me ! . . .   Father ! Thou
Hast taken from my heart its weight of woe ;
Hast rent the veil that shut the light of hope

Long from my spirit; hast lifted up the black
And terrible pall that lay upon my soul—
Transforming it to white and shining robes,
For the fair form long hidden from my view,
And given the dear one back into my arms
Thus panoplied in Light.   Thanks, thanks, oh God!
Adorable—Supreme—Eternal One!

Ah! not an answering tone from all the groves!
My joyous heart, that craves the sympathy
Of whatsoe'er is nearest, beats alone.
The flowers that were the glory of the spring,
The singing birds that made the summer glad,
And the green leaves that through the changing months
Danced in the sun and whispered to the breeze,
All, all have pass'd away.   The weary gales
Come sighing from the meadows up the slope,
And die in plaintive murmurs: in the elm
The jay screams hoarsely, and the squirrel barks
Where the old oak stands naked: from the leaves,
That rustle to my tread, an odor comes
As of mortality.   It is the sad,
Sweet period of the year our calends call
The "Indian Summer."   Beautifully pass
The seasons into this.   The harvest done,
The summer days round slowly with a hush
Into the quiet of the August noons.

Fields then lie bare ; the skies grow milky-blue;
The streams run lazily ; the tiniest child
Can jump the brooks, or wade them dry at knee;
One far retired in this wide Wood, can hear
Its deep heart throb, so still is every thing :
Out o'er the meadows, where from earliest morn
The grazing herds have fed, they quit the dry,
Hot grasses, and seek out the shadiest pools,
Where, plunging belly-deep, they thus await
The cooler eve's approach so quietly,
They look like statues from red granite hewn,
Or cast in bronze, or cut in ivory ;
The restless sheep are scattered, each with nose
Thrust in protecting grasses; by the bars,
Beneath the walnut shade, the horses dose
The mid-day hours away ; around the fields,
The groves are silent; dotting here and there
The faded landscape, like gray clouds at rest,
The old farm-houses lie; the lolling dog,
That ever claims the shadow of the porch,
Frets the hot noon through ; all is still beside.

The quivering flame of August noons, at length,
Burns out; and with September's equinox
The earth grows cooler, and the quicken'd airs
More freshly touch the cheek: but summer's breath
Yet lingers, till the still October comes

With frosty nights, and slumberous, sunny days:
Then falls the leaf; then fades along the fence
The golden-rod; then turns the aster pale;
Then fly the song-birds, by the robin led,
Whose voices through the summer months have fill'd
The woods with music, far to southern haunts,
In orange thickets by Suwanee's shore,
And Mississippi's broad magnolia groves.

Another haze now overspreads the sky,
That thickens into dark November clouds;
And soon, from where the stormy Saginaw
Lets loose the northern blasts, come driving down
Fierce wintry winds o'er wide and frozen plains,
Till drizzly days bring snowy nights, and all
Is desolate.—But vainly yet the light
And feathery flakes descend on earth, and cling
Upon the trees; for often still come warm
And sunny noons, which lift the thin white shroud
From limbs it prematurely wraps, and lay
The folded linen back from Nature's face.
—Again the sunshine lightens up the vales,
And sleeps upon the hillsides: heav'n looks love—
And earth looks gratitude—and all the air
Sinks to a holy calm, like that which comes
Upon cathedral aisles when the last chant
Of voices, and the organ's closing peals,

Die lingeringly away.   Another change
Now follows silently; and from the broad
And grassy plains, and from the fallen leaves
That strew the forest-walks, and from the hills
And from the streams, like incense rises up
A gentle, all-pervading, softening haze,
As quiet and as soothing as the prayer
Last breathed in life from holiest Christian lips.

A sweet, voluptuous languor, fills the air:
The sun is shorn of his bright beams, and looks
Redly and dimly down upon the earth:
The moon glows like a buckler, as she mounts
In quiet from the misty depths, which now
No marked horizon separates from the dome
That spreads above : the starry hosts are lost,
All but the larger lights, which dimly walk
The heavens alone.   The breezes of the night
Catch the last lingering sweets of autumn-time,
And with them bring the murmurs of the brooks
To lull the senses to repose.   The warm
And wanton airs that through the slumberous day
Steal gently up from southern climes, caress
The willing cheek, and fold the languid frame
In long embraces, and on couches spread
In sunny spots of silence, thickly strewn

With sweetest smelling leaves, lie down with it
In panting ecstasies of soft delights.

  Now all the woodlands round, and these fair vales,
And the broad plains that from their borders stretch
Away to the blue Unica, and run
Along the Ozark range, and far beyond
Find the still groves that shut Itasca in,
But, more than all, these old Miami Woods,
Are robed in golden exhalations, dim
As half-remembered dreams, and beautiful
As aught of Valambrosa, or the plains
Of Arcady, by fabling poets sung.
The night is fill'd with murmurs, and the day
Distils a subtle atmosphere, that lulls
The senses to a half repose, and hangs
A rosy twilight over nature, like
The night of Norway summers, when the sun
Skims the horizon through the tedious months.

  Now airs as warm and sweet as those that kiss
The blossoms of the groves in Florida,
Steal softly whispering through the woods, and crimp
The sleeping streams. New leaves of new life
Seem given to him whose evanescent years
Are rounding to a long repose. His couch
Is near the window wheeled, his weary head

Is bolstered up, that he may thus look out
Upon the hazy landscape, and inhale
The grateful air. Anon he feels his heart
Thrill with a subtle influence, that lifts
His thoughts above the world; and then his brain
Throbs with delight a moment, when he sinks
Silently back in beatific dreams,
That give his soul a foretaste of the bliss
It soon shall know in heaven. While over him
Whose life is in the vigor still of youth,
Comes a sweet languor, touching first his limbs,
Then creeping stealthily along each vein,
And spreading till he yields himself at will
To the delicious sense of life alone.

  Such is the "Indian Summer,"—named by those
Who hither came while yet the Redman held
Dominion here. No fabling pen portrays
This season's sweet, luxurious, transient sway.
Not man alone, though he in chief, enjoys
Its brief career: the summer-working bee,
Voluptuous in his tastes, is tempted forth,
And forages with skill; across my path
The hoarding squirrel springs with fresh-got spoil;
The winter birds discard the sumach seed,
And dry wild-grapes, and haunt the sunny nooks

7

That lure the worm and insect out, for food
Of daintier sort.   All nature seems to feel,
Throughout her frame, the genial influence;
And woods and streams, and hills and valleys, look
Praises to God, the Infinite, the Good.

Miami Woods! day after day, for near
A fortnight now, I've come at early morn
And loitered till the eve, from point to point
Threading the forest mazes many a mile;
Now sitting, like the soul of Solitude,
On a brown hill-side backed by naked elms,
Gazing into the waters of the stream
That kissed its base, of many shadows full,
As if they were futurity; anon,
Hanging above the vestiges of life
In the world's infancy, that strew the plains,
And dot the slopes, and crown the highest hills;
Then lingering amid the stately groves
That girdle in the broad white fields of corn,
Whose golden ears yet hang within the husk;
Then passing with the farmer's children up
From underneath the beech and hack-berry trees,
Partaking freely soon of wholesome fare,
And cheating the long evening in discourse
Of Boone and Kenton and the Pioneers,
Of Pontiac and Ellenipsico,

Of Logan, the heart-broken chief, of bold
Tecumseh and the Prophet, Raisin's red
And terrible massacre, and Erie's great
And glorious victory—then all to bed:
Next morn, with only thanks given and received
For all this hospitality, away
Into the rustling forest-paths again,
Deep-lost in admiration at the brave
Resistance which the Redmen here had made
To the encroaching tides that drove them back
Farther and farther in the wilderness,
And kindred admiration of the bold,
Resistless progress of the Pioneers,
Whose spirit hardest toil could not subdue,
Whom dangers daunted not, nor death appall'd.

　　The "Indian Summer" thus hath pass'd away—
The soft, luxurious days of indolence,
Voluptuous and wildering as a dream
Of Hafiz in the Persian citron groves,
Fann'd by the spicy zephyrs of the East,
And sung to slumber by the Bulbul rocked
In sweetest folds of the imperial rose.
—Now, from the stormy Huron's broad expanse,
From Mackinaw and from the Michigan,
Whose billows beat upon the sounding shores
And lash the surging pines, come sweeping down

Ice-making blasts, and raging sheets of snow:
The heavens grow darker daily; bleakest winds
Shriek through the naked woods; the robber owl
Hoots from his rocking citadel all night;
And all the day unhousèd cattle stand
Shivering and pinch'd.   By many a potent sign
The dark and dreary days of Winter thus
Inaugurate their king.   A summer bird,
I fly before his breath.—Loved haunts, farewell!

𝔓art 𝔖irth.

1853.

A YEAR ago—a little year ago—
How long I lingered in these quiet haunts!
The earth was ne'er more beautiful than then,
Day darkened into night so peacefully,
And night so freshly brightened into day:
But storm and darkness pass'd upon the scene,
And swept it like a scourge. A year ago,
A little year ago, the stricken one
From scattering shadows look'd out on that earth,
And brightened in its beauty. Her young heart
And mine took lesson of the night and day,
And pass'd like them each into either's depths:
But storm and darkness visit not the earth
Alone, to desolate and to destroy;
They fall upon the human heart as well,
And sweep it also like a deadly scourge.

1.

I had a little sprite whose name was Hope—
It sang glad songs into my eager ear;

But when most loved its notes died all away,
And now its songs are still'd forevermore—
Forevermore.

2.

I heard a voice, born of my human love,
Speak to my human weakness words of joy;
Each was as sweet as sounds of dulcimers,
But all are silent now forevermore—
Forevermore.

3.

I held within my own a little hand,
White as the moon, and it became as cold;
I pressed it to my lips in agony;
'T was then withdrawn—withdrawn forevermore—
Forevermore.

4.

I've worn a faded lily on my breast
These many days, these many weary days;
But now, by unseen fingers touch'd, it falls,
It falls away, and falls forevermore—
Forevermore.

5.

I held a beautiful and precious gem
Against my beating heart, for many a year;
But while most cherished it hath turn'd to dust,
And here I lay it down forevermore—
       Forevermore.

  Oh, many are the sweet and gentle flowers,
Caught by untimely frosts, that droop and die
Ere half their beauty has disclosed itself:
The dews of evening and the stars of night
Watch o'er and weep for them, and kindly airs
Bear them to earth, and lay them in repose.
And many are the pure and gentle hearts,
Untimely touched by Death, that render up
The hopes and promises of opening life
Without a murmur, and go calmly down,
Along the way of shadows, to the grave.
And such an one has just been laid to rest,
Here, where the hectic leaf of autumn falls
And strews the fresh-heap'd earth, and where the pale
And perishing blossoms of the year lie low.

1.

Birds of the greenwood groves, and sunny meads!
Whose voices ever fill'd her with delight,

Come from the mirror of the glassy pool,
Come from the thicket's edge where berries hang,
Come from each airy perch and favorite haunt,
And from your sweet and ever-plaintive throats
Pour forth, in soft and melancholy staves,
A dirge above the loved and early lost!

2.

Winds of the spring-time! ye that bear the sounds
Of far-off murmurs on your dewy wings,
And steal a cadence from the running brook,
That rob the insect of its hum, and catch
The harp's last note, still trembling on the strings,
Pause here a little while, above this grave,
And in the tenderest tones of all, breathe out
A requiem for the loved and early lost.

3.

Light breezes of the summer! wandering far,
Combine in one the many sounds of grief
Ye gather in your long and lonely way,
And wed with them all sounds of earth and air
Too sorrowful for other company,
And murmur them at morn and eventide,
And in the hush of noon, above the spot
Where sleeps in death the loved and early lost!

4.

Soft, sighing gales of autumn! from the brown
And melancholy meadows, from the gloom
Of rocky caverns, from the plaining woods,
That mourn the hectic leaf and fading flower,
From deepest hollows and from highest hills,
Bring all the soft, sweet voices that are born,
And pour the saddest plaint that ever yet
Was uttered for the loved and early lost!

Part Seventh.

1856.

MIAMI WOODS! once more, in pilgrim guise,
I seek your venerable shades. My heart
Is swelling with a thousand memories
Of her who, in her youthful beauty, roamed
The child of Nature here. The lapsing years
Came with their seasons redolent of bloom,
Abounding fruitfulness, and garnered wealth:
Chances and changes left their impress here,
On many a scene : the glory of the woods
Faded and fell where migratory man
Spied out the land, and chose his new abode :
The quiet of the sylvan Solitude
Was broken by unusual sounds, that woke
New echoes in its depths, as through them rush'd,
With arrowy speed, careering Power, that dragg'd
The freighted car, along whose mighty track
The monarchs of the forest disappeared :
Where the rude cabin of the pioneer
Lay like a shadow on the grassy plain,
Or on the wooded slope, when first her feet
Wandered in prattling infancy along

Meandering rivulet and bounding brook,
The trellised cottage with its crown of flowers
Appeared, and statelier mansions rose anon :
The hand of civilization touch'd each scene,
And changed it : even our last retreats were not
Exempt, but into far secluded haunts,
Whose natural beauty art could only mar,
The axe, the compass, and the chain were borne,
Dividing and despoiling : onward came
The multitudes who people now these plains
And hills, not as a calm-careering stream,
But like a rushing torrent :—Still, the love
Of Nature, in her quiet, far retreats,
Oft brought us to these old majestic groves,
That even avarice hath not yet laid low.

In this our long companionship with woods,
And waters, and the star-like flowers that line
Each rustling path, and the bright, wingèd tribes,
That give the incorporeal air a voice,
And all but an embodiment, she became,
To me, a part of every sight and sound
Throughout this wide domain. And on each breeze
That steals up softly from yon babbling brook,
Her joyous tones come floating to me now;
And turn where'er I will I see her form,
For every mossy nook and flowery slope

Is living with her image.   Here, where time
Has spared a leafy covert of old days,
We sat when last she visited these scenes.
The shadow of a mighty sorrow still
Rested upon her soul; but day by day
Returning light was lifting up the veil;
And in among these old familiar haunts
I saw the struggle memory made with doubt,
And viewed the gradual triumph.   Soon we left,
For other scenes that lay in sweet repose,
And golden beauty, where the winter's reign
Is mild, and shortened by a kindlier clime.

Once more in beauty came the blessèd spring,
And garlanded the earth.   We were away,
Mid buds and blossoms of the sweet South-West,
Seeking to strengthen still the nestling hope
That God again had sent us.   From her brow
Faded the darkness of its late eclipse;
And with the gentle, spicy airs, that oft
Stole up from the far Gulf of Mexico,
Bearing the sweets of rifled orange groves
And jasmine thickets, she drank in what seemed
To be a new and rarer life, and grew
Stronger and stronger, till her heart again
Yearned for the gloom of woods, the glance of waves,
The arrowy gleam of wings among the trees,

And the glad songs of birds. And hence we went
Out where the groves had a familiar look,
When she roused up as from a dream, and shook
With passionate joy. She held but slight discourse
Herself, as yet, but gave a willing ear,
And more than pleased assent, to converse framed
Of Nature, and the visible Universe,
Of Faith, and Hope, and Love,—and at the name
Of God, or Christ, would humbly bow her head.
To singing birds and blooming flowers she gave
Quick recognition, and her lips would part,
And her cheeks flush, when memories awoke
That long had slumbered. She would fondly pause
Where rippling waters made a soothing sound,
And where in crystal pools the bright blue heaven
Was mirrored, and the fleck of passing clouds.

But hope is vain—and human strength is vain—
And tears and agony and love and life,
All, all are vain. As transient as the spring
Were the fair promises that bade our hearts
Rejoice. The jewel still retain'd its light,
But the enshrining casket had been rent,
And might not be made whole again. She knew,
Ere yet suspicion had aroused our fears,
That Death with ruthless hand was cutting loose
The cords of life. Yet still through meadowy fields,

That stretched in quiet beauty to the shade
Of neighboring groves, whose calm retreats she loved,
We bore her often.   But her feeble frame
Grew feebler as the passing spring went by
With its cool airs ; and when the summer came,
She faded like a flower before its breath ;
And ere the first of autumn moons grew round,
She told us, as the sad and weary winds
Came sighing up the slope, that she should die.
We bade her hope : she looked up at the heavens,
To tell us that her only hope was there.
We told her God was merciful, and good,
And just, and that he would not call her hence,
So young, so beautiful, so loved of all.
A momentary shade across her face
Pass'd like an agony, and disappeared.
Then with a light upon her countenance
That awed us into silence, it became
So like a halo, she with steady hand
Drew in clear lines the far-off grassy slope
Where she would lie, beside the younger three
Who pass'd to death before her—traced a slab,
Whereon she wrote her name, and these few words,
"She sleeps in peace,"—then with prophetic ken
Inscribed the year below.   Ere many days,
Though sorrow came and dimm'd again her brow,
Without a tear she press'd our swelling hearts

To hers, and on the ashen lips of each
Printed her farewell kiss—then gave her thoughts
To God, who had her heart and all her hopes,
Breathing her life away without a moan,
Or audible sigh, and sank to sleep in death.

We bore her body to the grave she wish'd,
And laid it with her kindred. Earth contains,
In her enfolding bosom, few more bright,
More beautiful, more loved: and fewer still,
Who, taken in the blossom of their years,
So willingly, so trustingly, went down
To the dark chambers of the silent tomb.

Sorrow is of the Earth, and joy of Heaven.
The dust of what she was, is here—the soul,
That clothed it with a glory from above,
Roams now untrammel'd through eternal space,
Singing with angels round the Throne of God,
And in the fountains of perpetual peace
Bathing its shining plumes. Such is our faith—
And yet we mourn for her, and can but mourn,
She walked the shadowy shores of death so long,
And struggled through their gloom so patiently,
Only to close her little dream of life,
And lay the casket of her soul aside,
When the thick mists were rising, and the world
Spread out beneath them, bright and beautiful.

L'EnVoy.

———

MIAMI WOODS!—The glory of a Dream
Rests on and beautifies the Real now.
What unto me your friendly shades have been,
That will they be forever—even more.
A sorrow common makes a common bond
Where else there would be none. Ye have beheld
My human anguish, and my human joy:
Ye are the friend to whom, in after years,
My heart will oftenest turn, amid its toil,
And sorrow, and dismay: your bosom holds
What unto it was more than words can tell:
But hence my voice is silent in these groves—
I sing no more the beauty and the strength
Here traced in many a green and flowery line,
And standing in the arching majesty
Of temples whose gigantic pillars rest
In the foundations of far centuries:
I sing no more the passion and the pain
That here o'ercame me: the triumphant joy
With which, when last I bade these scenes farewell,
I went upon my way, all starr'd with light,
I sing no more forever. The sweet hope,

That like an angel sat beside my heart
And sang away its sorrow then, hath since
Gone down in desolation. That which was
The central harmony of all this song,
The beautiful young Life that to each swell
And cadence gave the spirit that it hath,
It is no more a bodily presence here,
It is no more of earth; and now the last
Faint strain of this prolonged and fitful lay,
Which but for her, and for the love she bore
These scenes, had known no second touch, must die
Into a murmurous sound—a sigh—a breath.

8

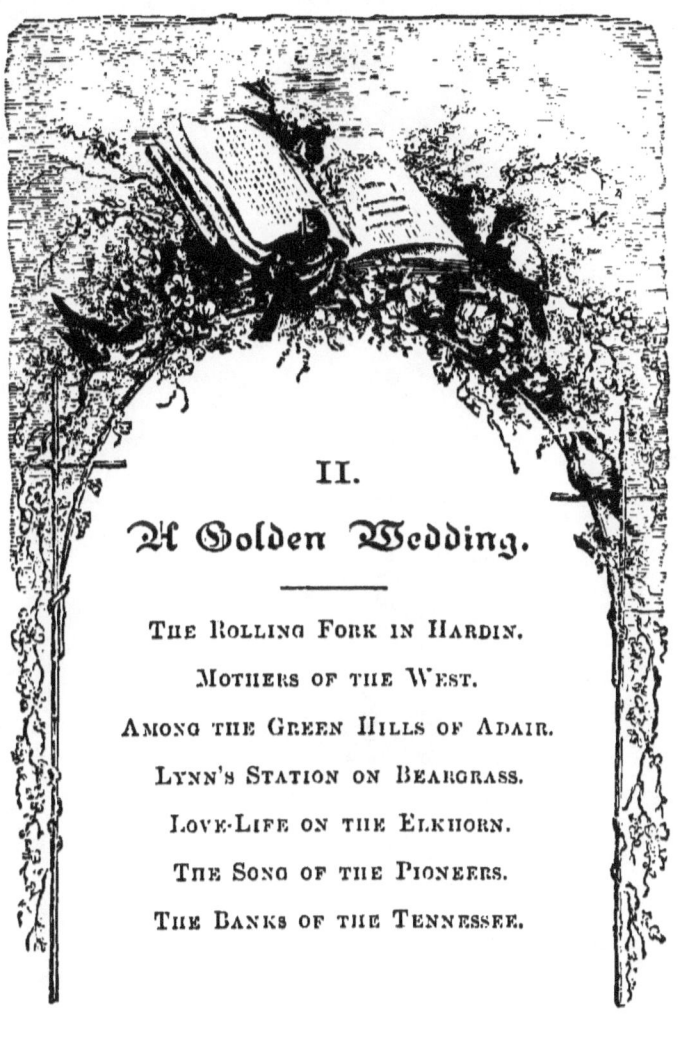

II.

A Golden Wedding.

A Golden Wedding.

THE ROLLING FORK.

I.

On the Rolling Fork in Hardin,
  Where the winds and waters chime,
And sing to the listening traveler
  Songs full of the olden time,
Stood a dwelling thrown wide open
  To the wanton airs of May,
That stole up over sloping meadows
  Which stretched from its doors away—
Here dotted with groves, there reaching
  To sunny and shady nooks,
Where the elder-bloom sway'd gently
  To the ripple of purling brooks,
And where the voices of children
  From blossoming thickets rang,
As, with jest, and shout, and banter,
  From rock to rock they sprang.

II.

'T was the home of an aged couple,   ·
  Who many and many a year

Had sown and reap'd and garner'd
    The fruits of life's labors here.
And now there had gladly gather'd,
    From near and from far away,
A merry troop of their kindred,
    And friends of an early day:
For this was their "Golden Wedding;"
    And the heavens stoop'd down and smiled
As sweetly and tenderly o'er them,
    As a mother o'er her child.
Songs of birds, and the breath of flowers,
    Floated in on the sunny air;
And God's benison seem'd resting
    All round them, everywhere.

III.

As friend met friend with greetings,
    How rapidly backward flew
The curtains of time, displaying
    The scenes of the past anew!
And soon they were where Lake Erie
    Heaved its billows like the sea,
And then by the moaning waters
    Of the battle-stain'd Maumee;
And anon where the bright Scioto
    Day's arrowy beams flash'd back,
As it water'd the Indian gardens

That border'd its shining track:
Then they saw the blood of their kindred
    Tinge the Wabash and the Thames,
And anon heard the streams of Kentucky
    Murmuring their honor'd names.

IV.

And as the lengthening shadows
    Of the years still upward roll'd,
And they talk'd of the days of their danger,
    And the tales of their triumphs told,
Tears gather'd in silent sorrow
    For some who had found their rest
Ere blazed in its fullness the glory
    That dawn'd on the Early West.
But they all felt proud of the heroes
    Who had sprung at their country's call,
For its flag, which they carried, to battle,
    For their homes, if 't were needed, to fall.
And the tears which had started in sorrow,
    And silence, were check'd by their pride,
And they still talk'd old times with the bridegroom,
    And recall'd still old sports to the bride.

V.

And while far behind on life's highways
    Their thoughts were thus tenderly cast,

One rose in their midst and recited
   This page from the Book of the Past—
One who, in the strength of his manhood,
   Had moved oft in the scenes now brought back,
And remember'd the WOMAN's devotion
   All along the Man's perilous track :—

THE MOTHERS OF THE WEST.

1.

The mothers of our Forest-Land!
   Stout-hearted dames were they;
With nerve to wield the battle-brand,
   And join the border fray.
Our rough land had no braver
   In its days of blood and strife—
Aye ready for severest toil,
   Aye free to peril life.

2.

The mothers of our Forest-Land!
   On old Kentucky's soil,
How shared they, with each dauntless band,
   War's tempest, and life's toil!
They shrank not from the foeman,
   They quail'd not in the fight,
But cheer'd their husbands through the day,
   And sooth'd them through the night.

3.

The mothers of our Forest-Land!
 Their bosoms pillow'd MEN;
And proud were they by such to stand
 In hammock, fort, or glen;
To load the sure old rifle—
 To run the leaden ball—
To watch a battling husband's place,
 And fill it should he fall.

4.

The mothers of our Forest-Land!
 Such were their daily deeds:
Their monument—where does it stand?
 Their epitaph—who reads?
No braver dames had Sparta—
 No nobler matrons Rome—
Yet who or lauds or honors them,
 Ev'n in their own green home?

5.

The mothers of our Forest-Land!
 They sleep in unknown graves;
And had they borne and nursed a band
 Of ingrates, or of slaves,
9

They had not been more neglected!
　　But their graves shall yet be found,
And their monuments dot here and there
　　"The Dark and Bloody Ground!"

VI.

The plaudits that rose from the many,
　　And the chatter that fell from the few,
Were silenced ere long by a trumpet,
　　Which peal'd out the "Red, White and Blue;"
And then, oft with tremulous cadence,
　　And tones that made holy the air,
From the hall came this song of a sorrow
　　Among the Green Hills of Adair—
The violin measuring fitly
　　The depth of the feeling express'd,
And the method and voice of the singer
　　Soon winning the heart of each guest:—

AMONG THE GREEN HILLS OF ADAIR.

1.

How oft in the spirit we yearn
　　For faces and forms that have fled!
While the calm lights of memory burn,
How oft from the living we turn
　　To the dead!

So my thoughts now go wandering back,
O'er a quiet and shadowy track,
Till they rest by a murmuring stream,
Where in years gone I dream'd a sweet dream,
   Among the green hills of Adair—
   The beautiful hills of Adair.

2.

And a maiden, as sweet as the flowers
   That bloom'd by that murmuring stream,
Walk'd beside me among the wild bowers,
Through the months, and the days, and the hours,
   Of that dream.
But a messenger cruel as Death
Broke in on that dream, and her breath
Pass'd away with a prayer and a sigh,
As that murmuring stream glided by,
   Among the green hills of Adair—
   The beautiful hills of Adair.

3.

But *I* wander there yet, and I hear
   The tones of that murmuring stream;
And the form and the face that were dear,
In the beauty of youth re-appear;
    And I dream—
Oh, I dream of a Land and a Life,

Lying far beyond earth and its strife,
Wherein, not again to be cross'd,
I shall find the sweet spirit I lost
   Among the green hills of Adair—
   The beautiful hills of Adair.

VII.

The refrain had scarce died to a murmur,
   When a woman well stricken in years,
Sang the song of Lynn's Station on Beargrass,
   In tones that brought many to tears:—

LYNN'S STATION ON BEARGRASS.

I.

As the clouds and the shadows are lifted,
   And roll from my vision away,
Lynn's Station appears on the Beargrass,
   With the green groves around it that lay;
And I see gallant forms and sweet faces,
   Such as brightened a day that is o'er,
And my ear catches faint and far echoes
   Of voices I'll hear never-more—
     Never-more—never-more—
   Loved voices I'll hear again never,
      Never-more.

2.

Now my mind and my heart, in their fullness,
  Wander back to the days that have been,
And my breast swells and throbs with emotion,
  Over memories of girlhood and Lynn.
Although dangers there threaten'd us often,
  Man's strong arm was a shield and a spear;
And woman's true heart made it stronger,
  As she bravely sang out, "Never fear!—
      Never fear!—never fear!
  Though the strong win not always the battle,
      Never fear!"

3.

And now I behold Nannie Allen,
  Who was kill'd in her maidenly bloom,
And her gallant young lover, John Martin,
  Who in tears and alone dug her tomb.
On a green grassy knoll, by the river,
  O'erlooking the Falls far below,
In the flush and the flower of her beauty,
  We laid her to rest long ago—
      Long ago—long ago—
  And the winds and the waves sang her requiem,
      Long ago.

VIII.

The tones of the violin lingered,
 As if they were part of the air,
Impregning the place with the holy
 And beautiful spirit of prayer:
Ere long, though, the murmur was broken
 By a resonant clarion blast,
And before the enraptured assembly
 The host and the hostess pass'd.
On their taking position together,
 The clarion ended its play—
And he sang then this song of their Love-Life
 In Kentucky's old Pioneer-Day:—

LOVE-LIFE ON THE ELKHORN.

1.

We met first 'mid the horrors of battle,
 While rang the red savage's yell,
Where some of our boldest and bravest
 By rifle and tomahawk fell.
She stood by the door of a cabin,
 Unshrinking, determined and grand,
From a loophole surveying the struggle,
 An axe duly poised in her hand.

2.

I bridled a steed that was halter'd
  In a shed that stood haply behind,
And pointing the way that was safest,
  She mounted and rode like the wind.
With night the fierce battle was over,
  And we cared for our wounded and slain,
Yet till peace spread its wings o'er Kentucky
  In beauty, we met not again.

3.

But peace brought the triumphs of labor,
  And scattered the shadows of gloom,
And the green fertile shores of the Elkhorn
  Soon revel'd in beauty and bloom.
And then, as if heaven-directed,
  We met where that cabin once stood,
And walk'd hand-in-hand where our heroes
  Had gone down in battle and blood.

4.

And we met there again, and there plighted
  Our faith to each other for life;
And never on earth yet has Heaven
  Dealt kindlier with husband and wife.

And in memory now we together
  Go back where that cabin once stood,
And thank God that soon out of the evil
  We witness'd and shared, came the good.

IX.

At the close came kind words and good wishes
  From all, that were fervent and true;
And the drum and the fife and the trumpet
  Pealed out again, " Red, White, and Blue!"
Then came, floating in from the porches,
  A smother'd and twittering hum,
And the young clapp'd their hands as they shouted—
  "The Pioneer Legion has come!"
And a dozen in buckskin-breeches,
  By hunting-shirts overhung,
Walk'd in under caps of 'coonskin,
  And saluted both old and young;
And they beat then the stately marches
  Of time, on the notes of the years,
As they sang, to a fitting melody,
  The Song of the Pioneers:—

THE SONG OF THE PIONEERS.

1.

A song for the Early Times Out West,
  And our green old forest-home,

Whose pleasant memories freshly yet
    Across the bosom come :
A song for the free and gladsome life
    In those early days we led,
With a teeming soil beneath our feet,
    And a smiling Heav'n o'erhead !
Oh, the waves of life danced merrily,
    And had a joyous flow,
In the days when we were Pioneers,
    Fifty years ago !

2.

The hunt, the shot, the glorious chase,
    The captured elk, or deer ;
The camp, the big bright fire, and then
    The rich and wholesome cheer :—
The sweet sound sleep at dead of night,
    By our camp-fires blazing high—
Unbroken by the wolf's long howl,
    And the panther springing by.
Oh, merrily pass'd the time, despite
    Our wily Indian foe,
In the days when we were Pioneers,
    Fifty years ago !

3.

We shunn'd not labor : when 't was due
    We wrought with right good will ;

And for the homes we won for them,
　Our children bless us still.
We lived not hermit lives, but oft
　In social converse met;
And fires of love were kindled then,
　That burn on warmly yet.
Oh, pleasantly the stream of life
　Pursued its constant flow,
In the days when we were Pioneers,
　Fifty years ago.

4.

We felt that we were fellow men;
　We felt we were a band,
Sustain'd here in the wilderness
　By Heaven's upholding hand.
And when the solemn Sabbath came,
　Assembling in the wood,
We lifted up our hearts in prayer
　To God the only Good.
Our temples then were earth and sky;
　None others did we know,
In the days when we were Pioneers,
　Fifty years ago!

5.

Our forest-life was rough and rude,
　And dangers closed us round;
But here, amid the green old trees,

Freedom was sought and found.
Oft through our dwellings wintry blasts
   Would rush, with shriek and moan;
We cared not—though they were but frail,
  · We felt they were our own!
Oh, free and manly lives we led,
   Mid verdure, or mid snow,
In the days when we were Pioneers,
   Fifty years ago!

6.

But now our course of life is short;
   And as, from day to day,
We're walking on with weakening step,
   And halting by the way,
Another Land more bright than this,
   To our dim sight appears,
And on our way to it we all
   Are moving with the years.
Yet while we linger, we may still
   Our backward glances throw,
To the days when we were Pioneers,
   Fifty years ago!

X.

The Wedding-Feast followed.— · · ·
  · · · When evening
Had quietly yielded to night,

The grove at the front was found blazing,
   Every tree with its lantern a-light.
And soon from a garlanded terrace,
   The viol and trump made their din,
Giving place, as the company gather'd,
   To the notes of the gay violin.
Then the Country-Dance answered with spirit
   To old Rosin's familiar appeal,
And Cotillions glode on, through the Gallop
   And Waltz, to Virginia's old Reel.
And the Past and the Present there mingled,
   As the old and the young thus met,
That day throughout life to remember,
   And that night never, never forget.

XI.

Thus ended that GOLDEN WEDDING,
   An hour ere the dawn of day,
On the Rolling Fork of Hardin,
   In the flowery month of May;
And before the bright sun had risen
   All the guests their couches press'd,
By the murmur of winds and waters
   Gently wooed, and lull'd to rest—
All but one, whom the chains of memory
   Held so firm in their thraldom still,
That a link ev'n had not been broken

By the waltz, or the lithe quadrille:
And from him, as the host and hostess
　　At length their chamber sought,
A low and tremulous murmur
　　Their ears for a moment caught;
And soon, as they paused to listen,
　　They heard, low-toned but free,
This song of an old log-cabin
　　On the Banks of the Tennessee:—

ON THE BANKS OF THE TENNESSEE.

1.

I sit by the open window
　　And look to the hills away,
Over beautiful undulations
　　That glow with the flowers of May—
And as the lights and the shadows
　　With the passing moments change,
Comes many a scene of beauty
　　Within my vision's range—
But there is not one among them
　　That is half so dear to me,
As an old log-cabin I think of
　　On the banks of the Tennessee.

2.

Now up from the rolling meadows,
    And down from the hill-tops now,
Fresh breezes steal in at my window,
    And sweetly fan my brow—
And the sounds that they gather and bring me,
    From rivulet, and meadow, and hill,
Come in with a touching cadence,
    And my throbbing bosom fill—
But the dearest thoughts thus waken'd,
    And in tears brought back to me,
Cluster round that old log-cabin
    On the banks of the Tennessee.

3.

To many a fond remembrance
    My thoughts are backward cast,
As I sit by the open window
    And recall the faded past—
For all along the windings
    Of the ever-moving years,
Lie wrecks of hope and of purpose
    That I now behold through tears—
And of all of them, the saddest
    That is thus brought back to me,

Makes holy that old log-cabin
   On the banks of the Tennessee.

Glad voices now greet me daily,
   Sweet faces I oft behold,
Yet I sit by the open window,
   And dream of the times of old—
Of a voice that on earth is silent,
   Of a face that is seen no more,
Of a spirit that falter'd not ever
   In the struggle of days now o'er—
And a beautiful grave comes pictured
   Forever and ever to me,
From a knoll near that old log-cabin
   On the banks of the Tennessee.

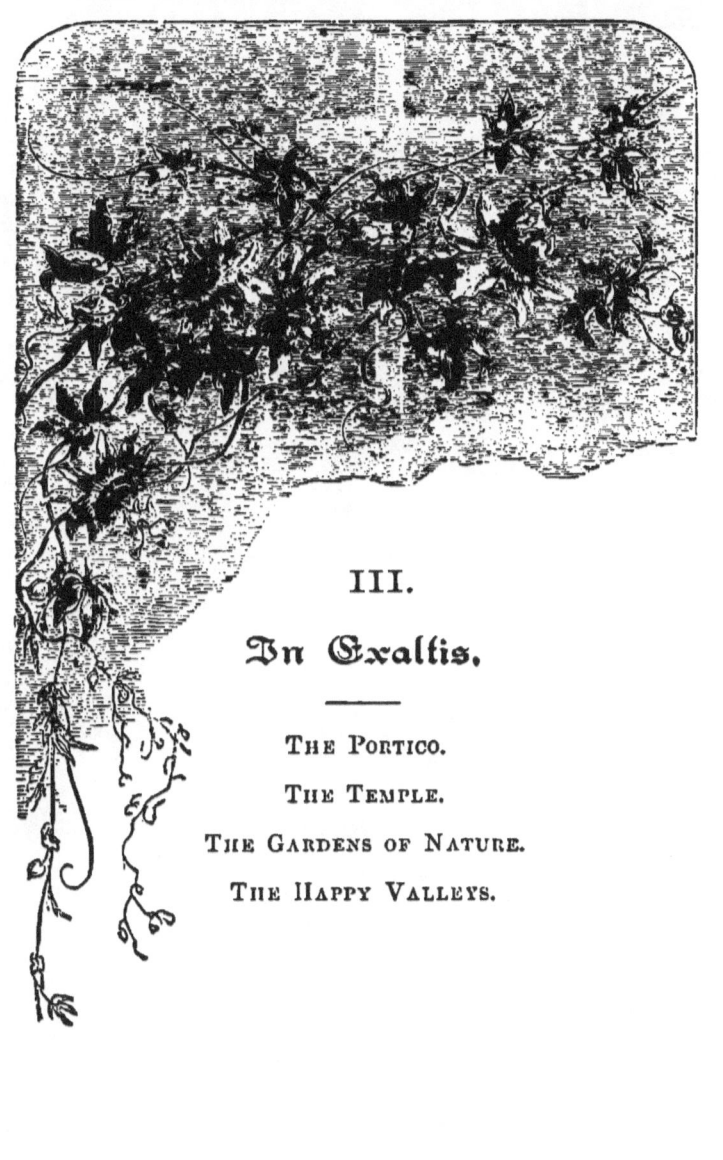

III.

In Exaltis.

I.

The Portico.

I.

There is a temple, not made with hands,
That out in the broad blue firmament stands.
From the silence and shade of its Portico,
I lookt out o'er the landscape that lay below :—
Green, meadowy reaches, in light that ran
To the edgings of brown where groves began ;
With here-and-there, now miss'd, now met,
The silvery line of a rivulet,
That up from its fringing greenness glanced,
As into the thickets and out it danced ;
And away, but indistinct and dim,
On the broad savanna's farthest rim,
Embowered in beauty, what seem'd to be
The dwellings of men, all tranquilly
Reposing in fields around them spread,
As calm as the heav'n that arch'd o'er head.

II.

And over the greenness, and over the brown
That fell from the groves like a mantle down,

Soon spread a mystical glamour, born
In part of the night, in part of the morn,
Whose soft, warm colors, drifting by,
Lay anon like mist on the mind and the eye;
And visions of wonder, half fear'd, half enjoy'd,
Floating up, sailing on, fill'd that mystical void.
As I lookt, still, and marvel'd, I felt round me fall
The gloom of the cloud that now rests on us all—
The wing of the shadow, the weight of the frown,
That in Eden with words of upbraiding came down;
And out of the distance and darkness stole in
Troubled sounds; and then o'er the bewildering din,
Breaking through the sweet songs of the brooks and
        the trees,
Rose this Wail, floating up on the breath of the breeze:—

WAIL OF HUMAN SPIRITS.

1.

Disenthrall'd, we yet linger: not of earth, we are here:
And we move in the Mystery yet—year after year.
Like a sunbeam from Darkness to Light we were born—
But our breath pass'd away with the mists of the morn.

2.

Like the grass of the field, ere the seed is yet brown,
We were markt for the scythe, and cut ruthlessly down:

Like the flow'r of the grass we were wafted away—
And the Night came before we well knew it was Day.

3.

In the Mystery still do we grope; and we fight
With vague shades in a void that ne'er promises light,
And yet never brings darkness: we linger, and grope,
And despair never comes, yet we never know hope.

4.

It is never so dark but that shadows we see:
It is light enough never from darkness to flee:
The silence oppresses, bewilders, confounds,
Yet less than the voices, which never are sounds.

III.

The air labor'd heavily.   Shadowy forms,
Like those that oft marshal the quick-coming storms
When Aries or Libra full-haloed appears,
And rules o'er the earth from the path of the spheres,
Came and went.   Then the winds, as appall'd, held their
    breath,
And the forms that they bore became quiet as death:
E'en the woods ceast to murmur—the brooks to rejoice—
And all life lay in trance, without motion or voice.
—Of a sudden, the cry of the bittern was heard,
And the earth in the breath of the hurricane stir'd:

Then the air for a moment grew thick, and again
The clouds, like a fleet of ships caught on the main
In the sweep of Euroclydon, wildly were driven
And tost like the sea-foam, until the pale heaven
Shone faintly between them, and smiled on the path
Which the hurricane's breath had just swept in its wrath.
Then quiet came back, and the sun, and the breeze;
And the brooks sang again to the winds and the trees.

IV.

Soon chants as of triumph, though not as of war,
Stole thrillingly in from the silence afar;
And this Song of the Seraphim, borne from above,
Where no mutterings of Hate mar the anthems of Love,
Took the place of the Wail of distrust and despair,
And with harmony fill'd every wave of the air.

SONG OF THE SERAPHIM.

1.

Up, where the King of Glory sits,
   Here where His People have their homes,
Never the wing of a shadow flits,
   Never the wail of a sorrow comes:
But the glimmer of stars, and the gleam of the sun,
   And the light that streams from the high white
     Throne,

Shine while the heavenly anthems run,
    Where angels the words of Love intone.

2.

Out of the mists, and above the din,
    Here, where the King of Glory reigns,
Never a shadow enters in,
    Never a troubled voice complains:
But angels sing the Song of the Lamb,
    Whereat the Trail of the Serpent ends:
And the Voice of the high-enthroned "I Am"
    A hope for man through the ages sends.

3.

Up where the King of Glory sits,
    Out of the mist, and above the din,
Never the wing of a shadow flits,
    Never a sorrow enters in:
But light and love, and prayer and praise,
    And charity that all invites,
Make up the measureless, endless days,
    The days of heav'n, that know no nights.

V.

And the arching groves responsive rang,
As the heav'nly chorists soar'd and sang;

And out of the soft South-Western Land
A freshening breeze came in, and fan'd
The mists to motion, and toucht the trees
To joyous and beautiful harmonies.
Then cloudlets form'd, and sail'd away
Like tilting ships on a rolling bay;
And over the landscape, erewhile dun,
Flasht brightly the beams of the slanting sun;
And the splendor and beauty of earth and sky,
Reflecting the Majesty throned on high,
Proclaim'd, as the glory spread abroad,
The goodness and power and love of God.

II.

The Temple.

I.

'Twas a beautiful, bright, bland Autumn Day.
A Sabbath hush on my spirit lay.
I had heard the Sermon, and bow'd in prayer,
And laid my heart to its Maker bare.
I had eaten the fat of the fruitful land,
And given God thanks for His liberal hand.
I had turn'd from Pilate, and sicken'd, to Christ,
And wept o'er the Life he sacrificed.
I had lookt on the proud, on the meek, on the lowly,
And thought of the Sabbath, "to keep it holy."
I had walkt with the Savior in Galilee
And felt doubt, and confusion, and darkness flee.

II.

Then I enter'd that Temple, not made with hands,
That out in the broad blue firmament stands.
By the "Rock of Ages," in its midst
I stood; and I said in my Soul: "Thou didst,
Oh God! this temple build for Man:
And in it he worshipt ere yet began

11

The pomp and pride of the synagogues,
And the boastful structures hewn of logs
And of granite and marble; and long ere yet
The mosque arose, and the minaret.
—If then and thus Thou didst let him bow,
And worship, wilt Thou forbid him now?"

III.

Whilst the waving woods, and the whispering breeze,
Fill'd the arching groves with their symphonies,
I rose; and I felt that the Spirit of God
Fill'd the Temple He founded, high and broad;
And I said in my soul, as I gazed up above,
'Tis a Spirit of liberty, light, and love,
And of mercy, and goodness, and beauty and truth."
And the Faith of my Age to the Hope of my Youth
Cried aloud: "Thou hast said it! 'tis *as* thou hast said!"
And again to that Spirit I bow'd down my head,
And I worshipt. "Oh God! if this worship be not
What Thou willest," I cried, "set thy sign on this spot!"

IV.

And I worshipt, and waited. I got not a sign;
But the Spirit of Peace rested on me—was mine—
And I worshipt, and waited. No Horeb—no bush,
Burning voiceful—no Sinai, with thunders. The hush,
Though, that came over nature, around and above,

Fill'd my breast with devotion, with rapture, with love—
And I worshipt, and waited.   Then came unto me,
In the depths of my spirit, with tones like the sea,
This only: "The Temple that arches abroad,
Over all, is the House of the Living God!"
And then this, as to Christ all the Centuries ran,
And this only: "The Sabbath was made for Man!"

V.

And I cried out: "Oh man! to the house of prayer
Made with hands, go up—for thy God is there;
And, in the days of thy beautiful youth,
Bow down, and worship in spirit and truth;
In the mightier years of thy ripening age,
There still against Sin in the battle engage:
But say not of him who goes out and stands
In that grand old Temple *not* made with hands,
And hungers and thirsts, and worships and waits,
And for righteousness longs and supplicates,
THAT HE ERRS: for Christ and his Cross are there,
And God's Angels come to him unaware."

VI.

Then I thought of Jacob, by Isaac sent
Afar into Haran, and then, as he went,
Of the ladder at Bethel, whereon in the night
Moved the Angels of God, in their vestments of light;

Of the Spirit, with purpose benign and strong,
That at Penuel met Jacob, and wrestled long;
And then of the Voice that so often spoke
To Moses, who broke the Egyptian yoke;
Of the Ravens that fed, in his sore distress,
Elijah prone in the Wilderness;
And the hungry hosts, that on manna fed,
And by unseen hands were comforted.

VII.

And I thought of the Dove that came to Christ,
When he rose from the water, by John baptized;
Of the Mountain of Light, and the Shining Cloud,
And the Voice that out of it spoke aloud;
Of the Light that arrested and startled Paul
On his way to Damascus down; and the call
That then shook his soul; and the thick, dull night,
That lay on his eyes when withdrew that Light;
Of the Tones that at Corinth bade him "Cease
Not thou, nor fear, nor yet hold thy peace;"
And of *all* sights and sounds, of the earth and air,
Which proclaim that—"God is Everywhere!"

III.

𝕿𝖍𝖊 𝕲𝖆𝖗𝖉𝖊𝖓𝖘 𝖔𝖋 𝕹𝖆𝖙𝖚𝖗𝖊.

— —

I.

I rambled o'er the meadow-lands;
  I walkt along the river: —
The sun was shooting golden shafts
  From out his autumn quiver;
The slanting arrows hit the waves,
  Refracted, and ascended,
Till in the shimmering air above
  With gathering mists they blended.
Effulgent glory clothed the sky,
  A billowy blaze the river,
And still the golden arrows sped
  From out their autumn quiver.
I thought of God and Paradise,
  Of Christ and the Hereafter,
Till rous'd by children, hurrying by
  From play, with songs and laughter.

II.

I mounted then the river hills,
  And lookt down in the valleys: —

The beech-trees stood in shining clumps;
　The maples ranged in alleys;
The gum here plumed the sloping way,
　With ampelopsis twinings;
While not far off the monarch oak
　Hung o'er the sumach linings.
The hill-sides, bright with autumn hues,
　Now challeng'd the near heaven,
Along whose curves the golden clouds
　To silvery shafts were driven.
But neither put such glory on
　As clothed the gleaming river,
Where still the sun's swift arrows set
　The gathering mists a-quiver.

III.

The frost had done its artist-work : —
　Bright leaves, around me falling,
Blent their low rustle with the tones
　Of distant voices, calling
The cattle from the fields below.
　I heard the sweet bells tinkle,
As homeward wound the kine.　I saw
　The ferns and mosses sprinkle
My winding pathway down the slope
　With more than earthly graces.
I heard aloft the freshening winds,

And saw below their paces;
And soon I felt my new-strung nerves
 With pleasure stir and tingle,
As banks of clouds, with sunset fill'd,
 Came blazing up the dingle.

IV.

Dazed with the beauty, long I stood,
 As 't were 'twixt earth and heaven,
And gazed with wonder. "And *all this,*"
 I said, "O man! was given,
In the beginning, unto thee:
 Yet thou didst scorn the Giver!"
No more. There was no more to say! . . .
 Far up the rounding river
I saw the city's steeples shine:
 I knew what lay around them;
I knew the people's pride and sin;
 I knew the chains that bound them;
And, turning from all this, I gazed
 Once more on earth and heaven,
As up from off the gleaming waves
 The freshening winds were driven.

V.

The sun set. O'er the darkening stream
 The twilight shadows gather'd;

No longer danced in light the plumes
   With which the hills were feather'd;
The cottages in shadow lay;
   In shadow lay the meadows;
And up the darkening dingle's sides
   Like phantoms crept the shadows.
From farms I heard the peacock's cry,
   The bittern's from the river;
The city's bells, I thought, rang out—
" Deliver! oh, Deliver! "
And *now* the heavens outshone the waves,
   The hill-tops, and the hollow,
For crimson glory sail'd the curves
   Where'er the eye could follow.

VI.

I took my homeward way.   In dusk
   It lay, far up the dingle;
And dusky thoughts I felt come up,
   And with my fancies mingle.
The cottages lookt brown: I saw
   The darkening shadows win them;
But, as I pass'd, the lights of home
   Shone cheerfully within them.
The barn-yards lookt like graves, which here
   And there white slabs besprinkle;
But, passing, I arous'd the flocks,

And heard the sheep-bells tinkle.
A wild, dark thicket, far ahead,
  Each step was nearer bringing;
But, when I reacht it, deep within
  Its heart a thrush was singing.

VII.

So, on I went. And as I pass'd,
  Each shade had its bright lining;
And to my heart I said: "Oh, heart!
  Now cease thy much repining!
If what thou wantest, cometh not
  To-day, await the morrow;
And if to-morrow barren prove,
  Still hold thee from thy sorrow:—
For it was sure the cottage homes
  Had lights within to twinkle;
And it was sure the folded flocks
  Had bells that soon would tinkle;
And it was sure the thicket's heart
  Would yet with song be ringing;
And so of thine! No more repine—
  But wait the Future's bringing."

The Happy Valleys.

I.

I sat, far in the evening,
   My heart and soul aglow,
With some cherisht tokens by me
   Of the crowded "Long Ago."
I had drawn them from recesses
   Held as sacred as my truth,
Some with manhood's shadows on them,
   And on some the lights of youth:
And I noted, as life's periods
   Came together thus from far,
That the brightest had its cloudlet,
   And the darkest had its star.

II.

My whole life spread out before me,
   Like a crowded map unroll'd:
With the free, wild, summery boyhood,
   The staid manhood—formal—cold;
All the dreams, that never would be,
   Though I nurst them, aught *but* dreams;
The realities—hard—flinty—
   And with iron in their seams;

The glad voices, that are ringing
　Even yet, like marriage bells,
And the low, sad tones, still telling
　What the dirge forever tells:—

III.

All spread out before my vision,
　And stole in upon my brain,
Till I lived my life all over—
　With its pleasure and its pain.
And I askt myself: "Now *was it,*
　To all others, or to you,
Worth the living, for the little
　It enabled you to do?"
And myself replied: "By Heaven,
　Not by man, 'are we approved.
For *myself,* I hold it ample
　To have lived, and to have loved.

IV.

"For 'all others,' the man liveth
　Not, whose judgment I accept.
Who assails me, let him show me
　That he hath himself not slept
At his post, when all around him
　Moved the foe that robs and kills—

The arch-enemy, who filleth
　　The broad earth with all its ills.
By the judgment that's of Heaven,
　　Though its vision may appall,
In my strength, or in my weakness,
　　I will stand, or I will fall!"

V.

To a livelier sense of being,
　　With this answer I was stir'd:
But the dusk within my chamber
　　Soon again my vision blur'd;
And the loved and long-departed
　　All came back to me again—
And the living loved were moving
　　In the bright and shining train.
Though my life knew many sorrows,
　　I had cause for much delight:
Yet my thoughts all took their color
　　From my chamber and the night.

VI.

And around still troopt the shadows
　　Of the living and the dead,
Till the voice of the last departed,
　　In the old tones, sweetly said:

" In the land beyond the living,
  In the light beyond the sky,
That is where the Happy Valleys
  Of the dear departed lie.
When the golden bowl is broken,
  And the silver cord is shred,
We shall meet there all together,
  You the living, we the dead.

VII.

" There are trials still, and sorrows,
  Where the Serpent left his Trail,
But the true and trusting spirit
  Will not falter there, or fail.
In the Book of Books 't is written,
  By the Light that is the day,
' But my Word, though all else perish,
  Shall in no wise pass away ; '
And that Word contains the Promise,
  That the weary heart shall rest
Where the Happy Valleys whiten
  With the Mansions of the Blest."

IV.

Life Pictures.

The Mightier Realm.

I.

There was once a Queen named Dido,
  In a realm of the ancient time,
Who sail'd the sea, right royally,
  With a purpose deem'd sublime:
But she sank to the deep sea's bottom
  The wealth of that ancient realm;
For her woman-sway was supreme that day,
  And her hand was on the helm.

II.

By the coast of a foreign people,
  In that reckless time of old,
Her anchors she cast—and to land she past,
  With a spirit free and bold:
But the royal city she founded,
  And builded, and peopled there,
Soon became the scene of a spirit the Queen
  Could neither control nor bear.

12   (137)

III.

So she parley'd for time to ponder;
  And the people soon saw arise
By the sounding sea, what proved to be
  An altar of Sacrifice:
And on this the hand that had striven
  To hold and controi the helm,
With desperate art thrust a blade to her heart;
  And thus perisht the Queen of that realm.

IV.

There is *now* a Queen named Dido,
  In a realm of the modern time—
A realm that lies 'neath serener skies,
  And with purpose more sublime:
And this Queen has a pet named Fido—
  A marvelous, mischievous thing,
Who proposed once to sail,—though he'd only a tail—
  And to take the Queen "under his wing."

V.

But she knew that she couldn't trust him—
  For he'd neither a wing nor a sail
To respond to the helm; and her beautiful realm
  Might perish thus in the gale:
Yet she allowed him still to advise her—
  And he workt on her fancy oft,

Till she thought she could feel the lift of the keel
    And see the white sails spread aloft.

VI.

The dog and the Queen one day were seen
    Looking very much discontented;
And it seem'd that they had quarrel'd that day,
    But the good Queen had relented.
Fido complain'd that Dido reign'd
    Too much in her own dominions:
She should look all about, and spread herself out,
    And then try *abroad* her pinions.

VII.

    He could hardly be blinded:
    She was surely "Strong Minded,"
And ready for self-abnegation.
    The world, quite benighted,
    Could hardly get righted,
Without *her* active co-operation;
    But if *she* were once *there*,
    —It didn't much matter *where*,
Nor much matter what the distance—
    All things would go right,
    Both by day and by night,
For no one would think of resistance.

VIII.

So the Queen took a notion, she'd cross the broad ocean,
　—This marvelous Queen named Dido—
And *with* her she'd take, just for company's sake,
　Her marvelous pet, named Fido.
And they two went to sea, right ambitiously,
　And big with their mighty Endeavor,
And raised the shout, as their sails swelled out,
　"Oh, Woman is Queen forever!"

IX.

She stood at the helm of her new-found realm,
　—This wonderful woman, Dido—
And steer'd the ship with a firm-set lip;
　While high on the poop stood Fido,
Watching the seas as the rising breeze
　Drave the vessel on before it,
But fearing a wreck when he saw on the deck
　How the wild waves tumbled o'er it.

X.

The Queen was brave; and, as on they drave,
　She grew stouter and stouter hearted:
"Blow high! blow low!" she sang out, "I'll go
　On the venture for which I started."

"But what of your course?" shouted Fido, hoarse,
   And trembling with great emotion;
For he felt the ship give a duck-like dip,
   As they entered the open ocean.

XI.

The Queen now felt in her broad bright belt,
   And her fingers made quite a rumpus:
"I have brought the chart, which I knew by heart,
   But I left behind the compass!"
"Then helm a-port!—or our time is short
   On this marvelous, mighty ocean!"
Shouted Fido out, as he glared about
   And saw nothing but huge commotion.

XII.

"Blow low! blow high!—through sea or sky
   I'll sail, and sail forever,
Till face to face I stand, in the place
   I sail'd for, with my Endeavor!"
Sang out the Queen, in a pause between,
   The wind's rage and the water's:
(So like the way, when from HOME they stray
   And its realm, of Earth's fair daughters.)

XIII.

Just then the ship gave a terrible dip;
　　Yet, when it came up, still righted;
But its sails were split, and in ribands slit,
　　And Fido yelled out affrighted;
And the Queen, though bold, was wet and cold,
　　For some icebergs drifted near her,
And she saw the mane of the Hurricane,
　　As he shook it, clear and clearer,
Then felt its dash in her face, and the crash
　　Of the masts, as they fell about her:
But her woman-form still braved the storm,
　　And her woman-heart grew stouter.

XIV.

Then struck the ship on the ice! . . . . The dip
　　Of an oar was all, thereafter,
She knew till her form lay quiet and warm
　　In a fisherman's hut; and a rafter
That met her dull eye, held her clothing to dry;
　　And the fisherman's wife and his daughter
Like angels sat by her, and kept up the fire,
　　And ministered to her, and taught her
The virtues and beauties of HOME, and its duties,
　　And the kindness that took in a stranger,

And gave her the best that it had, and the rest
  She required, and saved her from danger,
And death. And she swore, as she thought it all o'er,
  That never again would great Dido,
—The wonderful Queen of this wonderful scene—
  Be led into folly by Fido!

XV.

"I saw the white speck, as she stood on the deck!"
  Said the sailor, with honest emotion;
"And I wisht myself there, near the Hurricane's lair,
  For I know all his haunts on the ocean.
Had *she* known but enough to have given a 'luff'!'
  And close to the wind held the vessel,
Her bold woman form might have weather'd the storm,
  For her soul was full-up to the wrestle!
As she lookt at the foam, on each billow's dark comb,
  Her own hands by the helm-wheel bound her;
And she mockt at the gale till it split every sail,
  And the spars lay in ruins around her.
But what right had SHE on the deck, and at sea,
  With that beautiful form by the helm?
The hand fell in vain on the Hurricane's mane
  Which at HOME ruled a mightier realm!"

XVI.

The captain lookt mad at the first, and then glad,
    At the sailor's outspoken emotion;
And after a while he sang out, with a smile:
    "Now hear *me*, my brave Son of the Ocean!"
And he lookt like a man whose thoughts inwardly ran,
    Ere he gave them the force of expression;
For he shielded his bright, beaming eyes from the light,
    With their lashes, and made no digression:—

XVII.

"*I* find in Dido, and her pet Fido,
    The Woman *and her Ambition*:
The *one* that's *two*—the False and True!
    The outward, seen condition,
Of inward fires, and wild desires,
    That burn and tempt while hidden:
The mastering greed that yearns to feed
    On fruit to her forbidden:
The reckless haste to cross the waste
    Which man finds dark and dreary.
The stubborn will, that struggles still,
    Though foil'd, and faint, and weary:
The quenchless thirst that bids her burst
    Through all restraints e'er taught her,

That she may stand in some new land
  And drink untasted water :
The wish to go out to and fro,
  Beyond the usual ranges,
And there to see what can not be
  Till natural usance changes.

XVIII.

"My mind fills with regret, whenever it 's set
  On Woman and these conditions ;
For could she but adhere, in her beautiful sphere,
  To its holy and beautiful missions,
As I know in the main she does, and refrain
  From the world's outer toil and strife,
Oh, how much more bright with affection's light
  And love, would be her Life!

XIX.

"But the wild emotion that yearns for the ocean,
  Where Man contends with Might,
And the false ambition that seeks attrition
  With him, in fields where the fight
Goes on of parties, whose frequent art is
  Deception, and theft, and fraud,
Bring roughly down the beautiful Crown
  Of Peace she wears from God!

13

XX.

" With all this *not so*, she can sweetly go
On her missions of Home Endeavor,
And Man's heart sing out, as she moves about,
' Oh, Woman *is* Queen forever! ' "

Woman.

IN ACKNOWLEDGMENT OF A COPY OF "LUCILE," PRESENTED
BY A FRIEND.

I.

In the highways of Life, here and there, now and then,
Amid muslin call'd ladies, and buckram call'd men,
One meets, though the race is now hardly styled human,
A man that's a *man*, and a woman that's *woman*.
Such scorn not to drink of the waters of truth,
That flow, pure and cool, from the fountains of youth;
Nor reject, for roast beef and plum-pudding, the meal
Fitly season'd and served by the hand of Lucile.

II.

Lucile! oh thou sweetest of self-immolators
That e'er walk'd the walks of the world in French gaiters;
Thou purest of Sisters, and bravest of Nuns,
Thou should'st have borne daughters—thou should'st have
　　　left sons:
But failing of these—perhaps Life's lesser part—
Thou still hast left offspring that sprang from thy heart,
Having just enough falsehood truth's force to reveal,
And just enough art art's device to conceal.

III.

It is true—is it not?—that the beings we know
As the beings of mind, are the beings that flow
From nearer the sources of trial and truth,
From nearer the fountains of freshness and youth,
Than the beings of muslin and buckram we meet
In the gilded saloon, or the church, or the street.
The alembic of Genius from which they proceed,—
From the sickness and sin of humanity freed,
From the gloss of its crime, and the grime of its error,
From its frenzy, it fume, its despair, and its terror,—
Gives existence to purer and loftier lives
Than are borne to most husbands by most of their wives.

IV.

Then hail to Lucile! contemplate her! look at her!
And hail to the power that conceived her—begat her—
Took her out from fair Paris—from Baden—anon
Built her chalet far up the slopes of Serchon—
Fill'd her sweet eyes with flow'rs and her pure heart with
　　　chimes
From the bird and the brook, and the bee and the limes—
Bade the thunders to speak, and the cataracts roll
Their grand diapason through the depths of her soul—
Gave a voice to the pinnacled solitudes there,
That was just less than worship, and just more than prayer—

To the pallor of age brought the rose-bloom of youth,
Clothed the passion of Love with the fashion of Truth—
In the man of the world found and unmask'd the true man,
Through the mind and the might of the self-sustain'd wo-
    man—
Set a spirit afloat on the wave, on the breeze,
And a living soul gave to the lone Pyrenees.

V.

Ah, Lucile—Alfred Vargrave—Eugene de Luvois—
If well "put on the stage," what "large houses" you'd
    draw!
But as given to the page of Life's prophet, the Poet,
You draw better still, and the "trade sales" all show it.
From which I conclude,—as I'm certain I may,—
That the world has still *some* men and women who pay
Willing tribute to all that ennobles the race,
And due homage to woman whene'er she displays
The uplifting emotions, the purposes high,
The unchanging resolve or to do or to die
For the truth of the tongue, and the faith of the heart,
Which we feel were Lucile's—which Lucile could impart.

VI.

" Woman's strength is her weakness," men often declare:
Just as much—and no more—Samson's strength was his
    hair.

Woman's strength is her virtue—her will—her desire
For man as her Lord.   Not as something that's higher,
But stronger; as something to which she was sent,
To be bone of his bone, and, in full complement,
To be flesh of his flesh.   The old Edenal story,
In making which true is her pride—is her glory;
For making which true she has longings.   Her life,
Left at least incomplete without being a wife,
And a mother, looks lovingly forward to these
High and holy accomplishments, just as the trees
And the vines that bear fruit, forward look for the wall
Which the latter must lean on and cling to, and all
The soft rains and warm winds and bright sunshines that
      bring
In their train the full beauty that's born of the spring;
With the bud and the bloom of the former, that shoot,
And fructify soon, and accomplish the fruit.

VII.

Woman's strength is, her virtue—her will—her desire:
Man's weakness is, not to be influenced by her
High hopes, patient waitings, long labors for good
For herself and for all, half as much as he should.
Look at Alfred Vargrave—at Eugene de Luvois!
How keenly she felt, and how clearly she saw,
—*She*, the woman Lucile—while perhaps all were sinning,
All three, against fortune or fate, the beginning

Of troubles whose path would be strewn with the wrecks
Of love and of hope—irremovable checks
To all present designs, or desires—every-where,
In its course, folly, frenzy, defeat and despair.
She, the woman Lucile, saw it soon—saw it all—
Knew the lightning would flash, and the thunder-bolt fall—
Felt the shallows—the reef—heard the roar—saw the rock—
Gave warning again and again: but the shock
Came the same; and the dark and the desolate shore,
And the paths that led to it, and the water that bore
For a time the frail barges of love and of hope,
That so recklessly sail'd up the hyaline cope,
Were strewn with the wrecks she had dreaded, foreknown,
And foreseen, and foretold of.   All light was her own,
All prudence, all warning, all wisdom, all kindness:
But against her were passion—fatuity—blindness—
That knew not, that saw not, that heard not, that reck'd not!
And who, like to them, just such fate may expect not?

VIII.

Woman's strength is her virtue—her will—her desire—
That exalt her, sustain her, forbid her to tire.
The priestess of Nature, interpreting God,
She is like much that Nature spreads grandly abroad.
Yet she's not the strong river that flows to the sea;
Nor the wild waste of waves that engulph it, is she;

But the vine that clings close to the husbanding wall,
Having faith it will not be permitted to fall—
Neither it nor its fruit. She's the angel that brings
Down the jewels of heav'n to the crowns of earth's Kings.
Though unheeded so oft, she's the voice that to man
Speaks as not e'en the voice of an archangel can.

IX.

Woman's strength is her virtue—her will—her desire
For a love that is purer—a life that is higher—
A truth that is surer—a faith that is stronger—
A hope that is brighter—a charity longer,
And broader, and deeper, and oh! much benigner:
With an impulse that ever incites her to twine her
White arms and sweet purposes round what is pure,
And serene, and unselfish, and sinless and sure.
What the rose to the garden, the leaf to the tree,
And the grass to the plains, to man's mansion is she.
Like the sun to the earth—like the stars to the skies—
She's the warmth of his love, and the light of his eyes.
But she's more than all this: she's companion, friend, wife—
Without whom man might live,

         But—would living be Life?

The Maniac.

I.

"Who walks by yon thicket of hazel and thorn,
Her hair all disheveled, her looks all forlorn?"
" 'Tis Mary, the Maniac—harmless, though wild—
Her constant companion yon flow'r-seeking child."
"And what is her story?   I pray you relate."
" 'Tis simple—and many are doomed to her fate,
Or worse, for from *self* shrinks the bosom that errs,
But oblivion of thought is eternally hers.

II.

"Few words will suffice to rehearse you her tale.—
Once Mary was fairest of all in our vale;
And the bloom on her cheek, and the glance of her eye,
Shamed the flow'rs of the earth, and the stars of the sky.
But there came to our vale, from the sunny South-West,
A youth who beheld her, and fondly address'd.
He wooed her, he said, as a fair forest flower,
Which he long'd to transplant to his far-away bower.

III.

"He wooed her with looks and with promises dear;
He wooed her with words the most honeyed to hear;

He wooed her in gladness, he wooed her in tears,
And employ'd each expedient to quiet her fears.
He call'd her the star of his being, whose ray
Could alone gild the gloom of life's perilous way;
He call'd her the sun of his spirit, whose light
Could alone win him back from doubt's wildering night.

IV.

" He call'd her his idol, his glory—the shrine
Where he knelt with a worship was all but divine;
He call'd her,—for words to his false lips came free,—
All man could e'er covet, or woman e'er be.
Touch'd, conquer'd, she rais'd up the low-kneeling youth,
For she knew not that falsehood is smoother than truth;
And his words on her ear like a melody fell,
Till her spirit was bound in a wildering spell.

V.

"She listen'd—and gone were her coyness and pride;
She loved—and with his flow'd her heart's gushing tide;
And at once seem'd her whole glad existence to be
Lost in his, as a river is lost in the sea.
From that moment her life was a trance or a dream,
And as tranquilly flow'd as some meadow-marged stream
Which is lull'd with the breath of sweet flow'rs, and the song
Of bee or of bird, all the summer day long.

VI.

"But 't was like that same stream, had one wave of its breast
Been defiled at the fountain to poison the rest;
And 't was like that same stream, were its course in the path
Which a hurricane soon was to sweep in its wrath.
She awoke from that dream, to the light of the truth;
But in ecstasy still clung her heart to that youth;
For to him all her love, worship, rapture, was giv'n—
Her world now, her idol, her glory, her Heav'n!

VII.

"Oft they stray'd by yon thicket: a bird carol'd there
A song that sooth'd Mary, and wiled her of care;
And still, though six summers have journey'd along,
She roves to that thicket, to listen its song.
But I wander:—Weeks pass'd; and the Frost Sprite came
    by,
With iris like colors, all fresh from the sky;
And the leaves,—in one clear, starry night, all was done,—
Gleam'd scarlet and gold in the sheen of the sun.

VIII.

"Autumn vanish'd; chill Winter's approaches were heard;
And gone was the song of that caroling bird,
Which so long had enchanted the forest and glade;
And gone was the Wooer of Mary the Maid.

He left her with fear and with trouble oppress'd,
To seek his rich home in the sunny South-West,—
Where, he told her, he'd meet with their wood-chorister,
Whose song should aye 'mind him of first love and her.

IX.

"He'd a mother to win to his purpose, he said,
And a father to soften before he could wed;
But he'd leave ere their bird from the South should be flown,
And return with its spring-song to make her his own.
The winter months pass'd, in their darkness and gloom;
But the forest tho' bare, and the flow'rs in their tomb,
Were less desolate far than was Mary's torn breast,
For she heard not one word from the sunny South-West.

X.

At length, where the Winter King rush'd in his wrath,
Came spring, and sweet blossoms sprang up in her path;
And the leaf started out from each bud-burden'd spray
She breath'd on, while holding her life-giving way.
Then back to the thicket return'd that fair bird,
And again, morn and eve, its sweet carol was heard;
But the wooer of Mary, who with it had gone,
Came *not* with its spring-song to make her his own.

XI.

"Day pass'd after day—week on week journey'd by—
And a dark shade was gathering on Mary's blue eye:
Still Hope, sweet deceiver! supported her frame,
And flatter'd her heart, though he hid not its shame.
But the Spring pass'd away: and the Summer's breath blew
On a cheek which was sunken, and pallid of hue;
And a desolate bosom in loneliness beat,
Of tempests of grief and self-torture the seat.

XII.

"Mary's tongue was now fill'd with her false Wooer's name,
But the poison-lipp'd spoiler anear her ne'er came;
And she sank, for her grief knew nor changing nor check,
In body and reason a ruin and wreck.
She rose from her couch with an eye fierce and wild,
But gentle whenever it turn'd on her child;
And that child is the only companion she hath,
To lighten the gloom of her desolate path.

XIII.

"All else, though six summers have journey'd away
Save it, and the warbler of life's fairer day,
She shuns; but to listen that thicket-bird's song,
She wanders there often, and loiters there long.

And sometimes as sudden as thought does she start,
With fix'd eyes, and check'd breathing, and thin lips apart,
And looks all bewildered,—as if she had heard
A tone of the Past in the song of that bird.

XIV.

"But the spell passes off with a word from her child,
And she looks on it kindly, a moment though wild:
Then it leads the poor Maniac home o'er the vale,—
As now.—And such, stranger, is Mary's sad tale."
"A curse on the Spoiler!" I muttered.   "Oh, heaven!
Can *he* go unscourg'd while his victim's thus riven?
No! Passion's fierce tempests must rage in his breast,
And his heart find a hell in its sunny South-West!"

XV.

Oh Woman—dear Woman! how often betray'd
By the blandishments sweet that won Mary the Maid!
How often, too yielding! led on to prepare,
By one moment of rapture, an age of despair!
Beware! for the tones the most fervid and sweet,
Are oft but the mask of the deepest deceit,—
As oft the wild flowers that lure with their breath,
Conceal the coil'd serpent, whose venom is death!

Mabelle Golding.

———

" MAPLE GOLDEN," the servants called her:
  She was the wildest, merriest thing,
That ever rambled the woodlands over
  To search for flowers in the early Spring.
The March-rime, even, did not escape her;
  And when the April violets came,
Her eyes were filled with the hues of heaven,
  And her cheeks with roses were aflame.

" Maple Golden's come back, Missus!
  It's just three years since she went away.
No longer a girl, she is now a woman,
  And her beautiful hair is streak'd with gray.
But she's changed so, Missus! You'd hardly know her,
  She looks so weary, and seems so sad—
She that was never down in spirits,
  She that was always fresh and glad.

" The matter? I did n't hear 'bout the matter;
  I saw her only a little while,
Just as she left the car at the Station;
  And I should n't have known her but for her smile;

That is, at *first* I should n't have known her,
    And did n't—but when I looked agen,
And saw her fondle and kiss the children,
    I 'd a-known her among a thousand then !

" At first she stood like the marble statue
    I saw at Muldoon's the other day ;
Then the smile that all of us used to love so,
    Across her features began to play ;
And then, for just a moment, she buried
    Her face in her hands, and press'd her eyes,—
(They are not the same, but the stars are in them,
    As they used to be, and the blue of the skies,)—

" And half-look'd into the group of children
    That stood but a little way from her,
All of them wanting to rush up to her,
    But each afraid to be first to stir ;
And then she look'd them full in their faces,
    And caught them up to her, one by one,
And kiss'd them and press'd them up to her bosom,
    And named them—all but little Nun :

" Nun, you know, has come among us
    Since that terrible, awful day,
When, in the storm we all remember,
    Maple Golden wandered away—

Wandered away, no one knew whither,
 And only a few have ever guess'd why;
And none have become a whit the wiser,
 In all the time that has since gone by.

" *I* know, Missus! and al'ys did know,
 For I was where I could hear and see;
But I 've been good to Maple Golden,"
 She sigh'd, " for Maple was good to me.
And I have kept my own good counsel,
 And mean to keep it as long as I live:
Many have ask'd me to give them a hint just,
 But I 've no hint that I 'll ever give."

" Wont you tell *me* now, Phillis? *me* just?
 Soon your secret 'll all be out.
When and where and how did it happen?
 What and with whom was it all about?"
" No—I 'll *never* tell on Maple—
 Maple 'll never tell on me:
To such as I am it 's little difference—
 It 's *all*, though," she sighed, " to such as she!"

" Please do n't ask me again, dear Missus.
 Maple's wells of sorrow are dry;
I judge by her looks, and by her movements,
 But more than all by her burning eye.

Yet were this not so, Maple should never
    Have cause from me one word to fear.
I wish she *could* weep, but she shall not ever
    For fault of mine shed a single tear."

" Well, Phillis—when you left the Station,
    What"—" Missus, here comes Massa John.
When *I* turn'd away from Maple Golden,
    He stood near, looking sadly on.
May-be *he* can tell you something, Missus—
    Something I miss'd cause I did n't stay.
Mass John! *you* saw poor Maple Golden,
    And was looking on when I came away."

" Well, John—I can't get much out of Phillis—
    Has Maple, sure enough, come back ?"
" Yes—the poor thing wandered hither, somehow,
    But has gone again, on a darker track.
Things *do* happen so strangely, sometimes!
    Her father had been for a week in town,
And return'd on the up-train half an hour
    After she on the other train came down.

" I saw her standing and gazing wildly
    At little Nun, till she spied a charm,
Which seem'd almost to electrify her,
    By Nature fix'd on Nun's right arm.

At this she caught the child to her bosom,
    And gave it many a sweet embrace,
Smoothing its hair with her trembling fingers,
    And planting kisses all over its face.

" The upward train then stopp'd at the Station,
    Near where Mabelle stood with the child ;
And her father stepp'd from the car to the platform,
    And bow'd to a friend or two, and smiled ;
When, all of a sudden, Mabelle toward him
    With open arms and a wild look sprang,
And for an instant a shriek came from her,
    With which the air all about us rang.

" He caught her tenderly, and drew her
    Beautiful form up to his own,
And kindly and lovingly address'd her,
    But she answer'd with only a dying moan.
She was borne then gently into the Station,
    And laid for a little while on a bed ;
But ere I left"——" Oh God!" cried Phyllis,
    "And *is* poor Maple Golden dead?"

" Dead ere I left." " Poor Maple Golden!"
    Sobb'd Phillis ; " I know her story well ;
'Tis a tale of guilt, and a tale of sorrow,
    But a tale that Phillis can never tell.

Mass John "——"Ah, Phillis! *I* know that story,
  And I know of one whose robes are white
As he moves on earth, but whose soul is blacker
  Than the blackest shades of the darkest night.

" 'T is the old, old story, of woman's weakness,
  And of the perfidy of man!—
Go, Phyllis, at once, to Mabelle's parents,
  And offer to do whatever you can.
Say nothing of what you *do* or *don't* know;
  Help lay that blighted flow'r in the earth;
And all who know of Mabelle's Temptation,
  Will pray for her second and better birth."

Over "The Bridge of Sighs."

" Over ' the Bridge of Sighs,'
   Into the land that lies
   Under the brightening skies
That glow with the coming day—
   That is where I would go,
   Out of this land of woe,
   Whose evil I see and know.
It is far, ah ! far away,
   That land of beauty and light ;
   But I feel in my spirit the might
   That, cheered by its gladdening smiles,
   Can compass the weary miles :
   So, over the Bridge I go,
   Bring it weal now, or bring it woe !"
   She said.   And her voice grew loud,
   And her step grew firm, and proud
   Her bearing, and keen her look,
   As her self-will'd way she took ;
   And, giving but one glance back
   On the long and weary track,
   She pass'd the Bridge, and in pride
   Stood erect on the chosen side.

" Now *out* from the Bridge of Sighs
 Into the land of Hope,
With brightening heart and eyes,
 And a clearer horoscope !"
She said. And into the land
 Of Hope, with a quickening pace,
She went—and she took her stand
 In a sunny and flowery place :
A place that forever was bright,
In the morn or the noon or the night,
With the golden and silvery light
 That streams from the stars and the sun :
A place that forever was sweet
With the breath of the flow'rs at her feet
 That bloom'd, and adown by the run :
And she walk'd through the days and the hours
Of months, by the light and the flowers ;
 But Hope she then found was a cheat—
 Bewildering her mind, and her feet
Misleading, till day after day
She threaded the same weary way,
 Coming back with the shadows of night
 To the place she had left with the light.

" And now, from the land of Hope,
 I go to the land of Deeds :
Whoe'er with the world would cope,

Must lean not on broken reeds !"
She said.   And she fix'd her eye
On a beautiful cloud in the sky ;
 But that cloud soon moved away,
 And was lost ere the close of the day.
Then from the horizon afar
Rose a bright and a beautiful star :
 " By *that* I can travel right on !"
 She said—and she started.   Anon
It had changed so its place in the sky,
That she murmur'd, with tears and a sigh,
 " If I follow much farther its track,
 Whence I started I soon shall be back."
In the morning she fix'd her bright eyes
On the sun as it rose, and the skies
 That were gleaming with purple and gold
 As the cloudlets away from it roll'd.
And with confidence now she began
Every object around her to scan.
 But the sun, like the star and the cloud,
 Proved a foil to her hope—and she bowed
Her head for a moment, then gazed
At a tall cliff before her that blazed
 In the light of the moon, and blazed on
 Till the beams it reflected were gone.

That landmark went into her dreams,
   Through the long and the wearisome night,
With its height and its strength and its beams,
   And the shimmering sheen of its light;
And when the sun rose the next day,
It caught and threw back his first ray.
      Then, proudly uplifting her head,
      She gazed at it calmly, and said:
" Again I shall fix not my eyes,
   For guidance by night or by day,
On what moves in the air and the skies;
   But by objects that rise far away
On the earth, and by objects anear,
Will I measure my distance, and steer;
      And for that which is righteous and just,
      I will place my full faith and my trust
In a region of beauty that lies
Far beyond the thin air and the skies!"
      And she did so; and thence moved in pride,
Life's highways and byways along—
      Faith and Works being ever her guide,
Trust and Triumph her prayer and her song;
      And, o'ercoming earth's trials and strife,
      She *won* in the Battle of Life.

Song of "The Knitting Girl."

LATE in the quiet night,
   By the warm coal-fire I sit,
My hand and my heart both light,
   And I knit—I knit—I knit.
And sometimes I interweave
A thought over which I grieve;
And then comes a gentle gleam
Of a beautiful light, and I dream—
I dream of a time to come,
But my voice and my lips are dumb—
And I think of a time now gone,
And a walk on the terraced lawn—
But all these soon disappear,
With a smile, or a sigh, or a tear,
And, joyous or sad or oppress'd,
With the midnight I slumber and rest.

The shadows soon upward roll,
   —Both night's and mine,—and the day
Comes down with its open scroll,
   Which I read as it glides away:
'T is the same I have read before,

But I ponder it o'er and o'er—
'T is the same I shall read again,
In sorrow, or joy, or pain,
As the labor of life goes on—
But the goal will at last be won;
And I wait, as it comes more near,
With a smile, or a sigh, or a tear,
Now working, and now at play,
Never doubting the Better Day:
So here by the fire I sit,
And I knit—I knit—I knit.

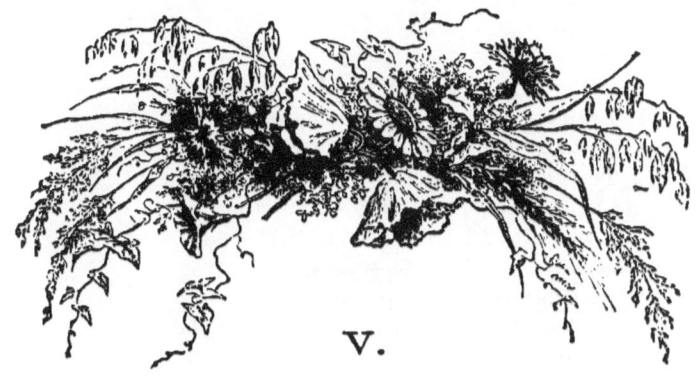

V.

𝔐iscellaneous 𝔓oems.

Proem.

God's holy angels, when the Earth was new,
   Ere yet green plant or golden grain had birth,
O'er the warm slopes and sunny valleys threw
   The germs of vegetation; and the earth,
As lapsed the seasons of the primal year,
   Grew fair and fruitful—yeilding, for all time,
The sustenance of Life—afar and near,
   On every continent, in every clime.
No quick return was part of this great plan:
But thus the seed was sown for all the Years of Man.

And, by this high and bright example taught,
   Would I thus labor in my lowly way—
Sowing the broad and shining fields of Thought
   With seed that shall spring up through many a day:
Not seeking quick returns, in wealth or fame;
   Not darkening counsel with unmeaning words,
Nor dazzling with a phosphorescent flame—
   But with a voice as cheerful as a bird's,
And with a hand and heart unaw'd by strife,
Singing and sowing seed for all the Years of Life.

The West.

———

I.

LAND of the West—green Forest-Land!
  Clime of the fair, and the immense!
Favorite of Nature's liberal hand,
  And child of her munificence!
  Fill'd with a rapture warm, intense,
High on a cloud-girt hill I stand,
  And with clear vision gazing thence,
Thy glories round me far expand:
  Rivers, whose likeness earth has not,
And lakes, that elsewhere seas would be,—
  Whose shores the countless wild herds dot,
Fleet as the winds, and all as free;
  Mountains that pierce the bending sky,
And with the storm-clouds warfare wage,—
  Shooting their glittering peaks on high,
To mock the fierce red lightning's rage;
  Arcadian vales with vine-hung bow'rs,
And grassy nooks, 'neath beechen shade,
  Where dance the never resting Hours,
To music of the bright cascade;
  Skies softly beautiful, and blue

As Italy's, with stars as bright ;
　Flow'rs rich as morning's sun-rise hue,
And gorgeous as the gemm'd midnight.
　　Land of the West—green Forest-Land !
　　Thus hath Creation's bounteous hand,
Upon thine ample bosom flung
Charms such as were her gift when the gray world was
　　　young.

II.

Land of the West !—where nought is old,
　Or fading, but tradition hoary,—
Thy long neglected annals hold
　Of many a daring deed-the story !
Man's might of arm hath here been tried,
　And woman's glorious strength of soul—
When war's fierce shout rang far and wide,
　When vengeful foes at midnight stole
On slumbering innocence, and gave
　　Nor onset-shout, nor warning word,
　　Nor nature's strong appealings heard
From woman's lips, to "spare and save
　　Her unsuspecting little one,
　　Her only child—her son ! her son !"
Unheard the supplicating tone,
Which ends in now a shriek, and now a deep death-groan !

III.

Land of the West!—green Forest-Land!
  Thine early day for deeds is famed
Which in historic page shall stand
  Till bravery is no longer named.
Thine early day!—it nursed a band
  Of men who ne'er their lineage shamed;
The iron-nerved, the bravely good,
Who neither spared nor lavish'd blood—
  Aye *ready*, morn, or night, or noon;
Fleet in the race, firm in the field,
Their sinewy arms their only shield—
Courage to Death alone to yield:
  The men of Daniel Boone!
Their dwelling place—the "good green wood,"
  Their favorite haunts—the lone arcade,
The murmuring and majestic flood,
  The deep and solemn shade:
Where came to them the Word of God,
When Storm and Darkness were abroad,
  Breath'd in the thunder's voice aloud,
  And writ in lightning on the cloud.
And thus they lived: the dead leaves oft,
  Heap'd by the playful winds, their bed;
Nor ask'd they couch more warm or soft,
  Nor pillow for the head,
Other than fitting root or stone,

With the scant wood-moss overgrown.
Heroic band!—But they have pass'd
   As pass the stars at rise of sun,—
Melting into the ocean vast
   Of Time, and sinking, one by one;
Yet lingering here and there a few,
As if to take a last, long view,
Of the domain they won in strife
With foes who battled to the knife.
   Peace be to those who sleep beneath us!
All honor to the few that yet do linger with us!

IV.

Land of the West!—thine early prime
Fades in the flight of hurrying Time;
Thy noble forests fall, as sweep
Europa's myriads o'er the Deep;
And thy broad plains, with welcome warm,
Receive the onward-pressing swarm:
On mountain height, in lowly vale,
   By quiet lake, or gliding river,—
Wherever sweeps the chainless gale,
   Onward sweep they forever.
Oh, may they come with hearts that ne'er
Can bend a tyrant's chain to wear;
With souls that would indignant turn,
And proud oppression's minions spurn;

With nerves of steel, and words of flame,
To strike and scar the wretch who'd bring our land to
    shame!

V.

Land of the West!—beneath the Heaven
  There's not a fairer, lovelier clime;
Nor one to which was ever given
  A destiny more high, sublime.
From Alleghany's base to where
  Our Western Andes prop the sky—
The home of Freedom's hearts is there,
  And o'er it Freedom's eagles fly.
And here,—should e'er Columbia's land
  Be rent with fierce intestine feud,—
Shall Freedom's latest cohorts stand,
  Till Freedom's eagles sink in blood,
And quench'd are all the stars that now her banners stud.

A Hymn of the Day that is Dawning.

——— —

If the promise of the Present
  Be not a hollow cheat,
If true-hearted men and women
  Prove faithful and discreet,
If none falter who are hoping
  And contending for the Right,
Then a time is surely coming,
  As a day-beam from the night—

When the landless shall have foothold
  In fee upon the soil,
And for his wife and little ones
  Bend to his willing toil:
When the wanderer, no longer
  In sorrow forced to roam,
Shall see around him spring and bloom
  The blessèd things of Home:
When the poor and widowed mother
  Shall fit recompense obtain,

For her days and nights of toiling,
  From the sordid man of gain :
When the brawny limbs of labor,
  And the hard and horny hand,
For their strivings, for their doings,
  Meet honor shall command :
When suffering hearts that struggle
  In silence, and endure,
Shall receive, unsought, the earnest
  Ministrations of the pure :
When the master with his bondmen
  For a price shall divide the soil,
And the slave, at last enfranchised,
  Shall go singing to his toil :
When the bloody trade of the soldier
  Shall lose its olden charm,
And the sickle hand be honored more
  Than the sword and the red right-arm :
When tolerance and truthfulness
  Shall not be under ban,
And the fiercest foe and deadliest
  Man knows, shall not be man.

Be firm, and be united,
  Ye who war against the wrong !
Though neglected, though deserted,
  In your purpose still be strong !

To the faith and hope that move ye
  In the things ye dare and do,
Though the world rise up against ye
  Be resolute—be true!

Truth and Freedom.

On the page that is Immortal,
　We the pregnant promise see:
" Ye shall know the TRUTH, my people,
　And the Truth shall make you free."

For the Truth, then, let us battle,
　Whatsoever fate betide!
Long the boast that we are Freemen,
　We have made, and published wide.

He who has the Truth, and keeps it,
　Keeps what not to him belongs;
But performs a selfish action,
　Which his fellow-mortal wrongs.

He who seeks the Truth, and trembles
　At the dangers he must brave,
Is not fit to be a Freeman :—
　He, at best, is but a slave.

He who hears the truth, and places
　Its high promptings under ban,
Long may boast of all that's manly,
　But can never *be* a MAN.

Friend, this simple lay who readest,
  Be not thou like either of them;
But to Truth give utmost freedom,
  And the tide it raises, stem.

Bold in speech, and brave in action,
  Be forever!—Time will test,
Of the free-soul'd and the slavish,
  Which fulfills life's mission best.

Be thou like the noble Ancient—
  Scorn the threat that bids thee fear;
Speak!—no matter what betide thee;
  Let them strike, but *make* them hear!

Be thou like the first apostles—
  Be thou like heroic Paul:
If a free thought seek expression,
  Speak it boldly!—speak it all!

Face thine enemies—accusers;
  Scorn the prison, rack, or rod!
And, if thou hast TRUTH to utter,
  Speak! and leave the rest to God.

Conservatism.

THE Owl, he fareth well
  In the shadows of the night;
And it puzzleth him to tell
  Why the Eagle loves the light.

Away he floats—away,
  From the forest dim and old,
Where he pass'd the gairish day:—
  The night doth make him bold!

The wave of his downy wing,
  As he courses round about,
Disturbs no sleeping thing
  That he findeth in his route.

The moon looks o'er the hill,
  And the vale grows softly light;
And the cock, with greeting shrill,
  Wakes the echoes of the night.

But the moon—he knoweth well
  Its old familiar face;
And the cock—it doth but tell,
  Poor fool! its resting place.

And as still as the spirit of Death
　On the air his pinions play;—
There's not the noise of a breath
　As he grapples with his prey.

Oh, the shadowy Night for him!
　It bringeth him fare and glee;
And what cares he how dim
　For the Eagle it may be?

It clothes him from the cold,
　It keeps his larders full;
And he loves the darkness old,
　To the Eagle all so dull.

But the dawn is in the East—
　And the shadows disappear;
And at once his timid breast
　Feels the presence of a fear.

He resists;—but all in vain!
　The clear Light is not for him;
So he hastens back again
　To the forest old and dim.

Through his head strange fancies run;
　For he can not comprehend
Why the moon, and then the sun,
　Up the heavens should ascend,—

When the old and quiet Night,
  With its shadows dark and deep,
And the half-revealing light
  Of its stars, he'd ever keep.

And he hooteth loud and long:—
  But the Eagle greets the day,
And, on pinions bold and strong,
  Like a roused Thought, sweeps away!

The Laborer.

STAND UP—erect!   Thou hast the form
   And likeness of thy God!—who more?
A soul as dauntless 'mid the storm
Of daily life, a heart as warm
   And pure as breast e'er bore.

What then?—Thou art as true a MAN
   As moves the human mass among;
As much a part of the Great Plan
That with Creation's dawn began,
   As any of the throng.

Who is thine enemy?—the high
   In station, or in wealth the chief?
The great, who coldly pass thee by,
With proud step and averted eye?
   Nay! nurse not such belief.

If true unto thyself thou wast,
   What were the proud one's scorn to thee?
A feather, which thou mightest cast
Aside, as idly as the blast
   The light leaf from the tree.

No:—uncurbed passions—low desires—
　Absence of noble self-respect—
Death, in the breast's consuming fires,
To that high nature which aspires
　Forever, till thus checked :

These are thine enemies—thy worst;
　They chain thee to thy lowly lot—
Thy labor and thy life accurst.
Oh, stand erect! and from them burst,
　And longer suffer not !

Thou art thyself thine enemy !
　The great !—what better they than thou ?
As theirs, is not thy will as free ?
Has God with equal favors thee
　Neglected to endow ?

True, wealth thou hast not : 'tis but dust !
　Nor place, uncertain as the wind !
But that thou hast which, with thy crust
And water, may despise the lust
　Of both—a noble mind.

With this, and passions under ban,
　True faith, and holy trust in God,
Thou art the peer of any man.
Look up, then—that thy little span
　Of life may be well trod !

Radicálos.

In the far and fading ages
    Of the younger days of earth,
When man's aspirations quicken'd,
    And his passions had their birth—
When first paled his glorious beauty,
    And his heart first knew unrest,
As he yielded to the tempter
    That inflamed and fill'd his breast—
When the Voice that was in Eden
    Echoed through his startled soul,
And he heard rebuking anthems
    Through the heavenly arches roll—
When he fell from the high promise
    Of his being's blessèd morn,
To a night of doubt and struggle—
    Radicálos then was born.

Through the ages long and dreary
    That since then have dawn'd on earth,
Man has had but feeble glimpses
    Of the glory of his birth:
Catching these, his soul, aspiring
    To its morning light again,

Hard has upward toil'd, and often
    Fill'd with hope, but still in vain.
Many a blessèd song comes stealing
    Downward from the Eden aisles,
Whence the light of heavenliest beauty
    Still upon the banish'd smiles ;
But the harmonies are broken
    Of each sounding choral hymn,
And the gloom that vails his spirit
    Makes e'en heavenly splendor dim.

Faint revealings, thwarted hopings,
    Wearying struggles, day by day :—
So the long and dreary ages
    Of his life have worn away.
War, and rapine, and oppression,
    Early in his course he found—
Brother against brother striving—
    By the few the many bound.
And in patience, and in meekness,
    To the galling chain resign'd,
Thus the fettered limbs have rested—
    Thus hath slept the darkened mind.
But it wakens now !—it flashes
    Like the lightning ere the rain ;
And those limbs grow strong !—when ready,
    They can rend the mightiest chain.

Through the slow and stately marches
   Of the centuries sublime,
Radicalos hath been strengthening
   For the noblest work of Time;
And he comes upon the Present
   Like a god in look and mien,
With composure high surveying
   All the tumult of the scene:
Where obey the fettered millions;
   Where command the fettering few;
Where the chain of wrong is forging,
   With its red links hid from view;
And he standeth by the peasant,
   And he standeth by the lord,
And he shouts "Your rights are equal!"
   Till earth startles at the word.

He hath seen the record written,
   From the primal morn of man,
In the blood of battling nations
   O'er ensanguined plains that ran;
In the tears of the deluded,
   In the sweat of the oppress'd
From Ind's farthest peopled borders
   To the new worlds of the West.

And he cometh with deliverance!
  And his might shall soon be known,
Where the wrong'd rise up for justice,
  And the wrongers lie o'erthrown.

Woe! the pride that then shall scorn him:
  He will bring it fitly low!
Woe! the arm that shall oppose him:
  He will cleave it at a blow!
Woe! the hosts that shall beset him:
  He will scatter them abroad!
He will strike them down forever!
  Radicálos is of God.

The Artisan.

THE day is past;—the quiet night
  Toward its midhour weareth on ;
His workshop has been closed for hours—
  A good day's labor done.
The toil is hard that brings him bread ;
  And sometimes he has scant supply :
When droops awhile his manly head,
  And glistens his full eye.

Yet from the trial shrinks he not ;
  For he has youth, and strength, and will ;
And though his toil is ill repaid,
  Bends daily to it still.
He sometimes murmurs,—but his pride
  Checks each expression at its birth,—
That blessings to his class denied
  Surround the drones of earth.

He passes, morn and noon and night,
  The homes of luxury and wealth ;
And glances at their gilded ease,
  His eye will take by stealth.

And shadows gather on his face,
    At times—but instantly depart—
He feels such weakness a disgrace
    Both to his head and heart.

His calling sometimes takes him where
    Wealth, worth, grace, beauty, all unite;
And lovely tones arrest his ear,
    And lovely looks his sight;
And much he thinks—and half he sighs—
    Yet ere his welcome work is done,
He longs for home, and Mary's eyes,
    And for his prattling son.

His labor hath been light to-day;
    And wife and child before him sleep;
And he has pass'd the half-spent night
    In study close and deep.
The lamp burns dim—the fire is low—
    The book is closed wherein he read;
But wildly swell the streams of thought
    Its fountain-pages fed.

With eyes fixed calmly on the floor,
    But varying and expressive face,
He cons the lesson o'er and o'er—
    The history of his race.

And much he finds of word and deed,
    Whose virtue is example now;
But more that makes his bosom bleed,
    And darkens o'er his brow.

The thirst for wealth,—the strife for power—
    The ceaseless struggle for renown—
The daring that hath seized a realm,
    Or caught a wavering crown—
The manhood that hath tamely bent
    And fall'n beneath tyrannic sway—
The balk'd resistance, that hath lent
    Its darkness to the day.

But chiefly this it is that fills
    The swelling volume of his mind:
The countless wrongs and cruelties
    That have oppress'd his kind.
And viewing them, upon his brain
    His own hard struggles darkly throng;
And as he feels their weight again,
    It presses like a wrong:

Wrong to himself, and wrong to all
    Who bear the burdens he hath borne:
"A yoke!" up starting he exclaims,
    "And oh, how meekly worn!"

But as he reads Life's riddle still,
  He feels, with sudden change of mood,
The stern, the indomitable will,
  That never was subdued.

The will, not to destroy, but build!
  Not the blind Might of old renown,
Which took the pillars in its grasp,
  And shook the temple down—
But that whose patient energy
  Works ever upward, without rest,
Until the pierced and parted sea
  Rolls from its coral breast.

In the dim fire-light, for awhile,
  His tall form moveth to and fro;
Then by the couch of those he loves
  He stops, and bendeth low.
Oh, holy love! oh, blessèd kiss!
  Ye ask not splendor—bide not pow'r—
But in a humble home like this,
  Ye have your triumph hour!

He sleeps—but even on his dreams
  Obtrudes the purpose of his soul;
He wanders where the living streams
  Of knowledge brightly roll;

And where men win their own good ways,
    Not yield to doubt or dark despair,
In dreams his bounding spirit strays—
    In dreams he triumphs there.

With stronger arm, with mightier heart,
    Than he hath felt or known before,
When comes the morrow's hour of toil,
    He'll leave his humble door.
No wavering hence he'll know—no rest,
    Until the new-seen goal be won;
But firm, and calm, and self-possess'd,
    Bear resolutely on.

And this it is that, year by year,
    Through which nor faith nor hope grows less,
Pursued, shall crown his high career
    With honor and success.
This—this it is that marks *the man!*
    Dare thou, then, 'neath whose studious eye
This lesson lies, rouse up at once,
    And on thyself rely!

Give to thy free soul freest thought;
    And whatsoe'er it prompts thee do,
That manfully, year in, year out,
    With all thy might pursue.

What though thy name may not be heard
   Afar, or shouted through the town,
Thou 'lt win a higher meed of praise,
   A worthier renown.

Press on, then!—earth has need of thee!
   The metal at the forge is red;
The ax is rusting by the tree;
   The grain hangs heavy in the head.
Heed not who works not—*labor thou!*
   Lay bravely hold, nor pause, nor shrink!
Life's Rubicon is here—and stand
   Not dubious on the brink!

The New Age.

———

RESPECTFULLY INSCRIBED TO THE REPRESENTATIVES OF
THE INDUSTRIES OF THE UNITED STATES.

———

As, to one who stands a watcher by the solemn-sounding
    sea,
Rise from the elliptic waters mighty ships continually,
With the race whose type is constant, though its outer-
    seemings range,
As the civilizations widen, o'er the boundless fields of
    change:

So, to one who gazes thoughtful, from the lessening shores
    of time,
O'er Eternity's expanses, silent, limitless, sublime,
Rise the marvelous, mighty ages, rounding up the shadowy
    spheres,
With the eternal laws of order, and the changes of the
    years.

Standing where the graceful vessel cleaves the ocean and
    the sky,
Where the starr'd and mighty centuries sweep with match-
    . less grandeur by,
Let me, while upon my vision coming changes brightly
    throng,
Sing the age's Jubilate—sing the Worker's Triumph Song.

JUBILATE.

I.

Hearken, human brother—ho!
   Worker at the board or bench.
High aloft the window throw—
   Let escape the stew and stench;
Air like that in these shut rooms,
Foul and damp with lingering glooms,
Do the best with it you can,
Is not fit for lungs of man.
Though the walls that rise about
Shut the blessèd sunlight out,
Yet the sweet and liberal air
Wanders freely everywhere.
'Mid the darkness, 'mid the din,
Lift the sash, and let it in!

Thick upon your pallid brow
Stand the reeking sweat-drops now:
Thicker still upon your face
Lines of anguish interlace.
Wipe away the honest sweat;
Proud of it you shall be yet!
Banish, too, the lines of pain—
Human toil is not in vain!
Work and wait—'t will yet be Day;
Long the task, but work away!

II.

Striker at the anvil, ho!
　　You are all begrimed and hot;
Still you strike a mighty blow;
　　Let your spirit falter not!
Brace your sinews—plant your foot—
White the skin beneath the soot:
Turn the iron—strike it well—
Every blow at last will tell.
Soon your clear or subtle thought
In the metal shall be wrought;
Soon the forge's glowing heat,
And the hammer's ringing beat,
So shall shape the iron rod
That 't will work for man and God;

So, too, shall your blow on blow
Bring the hour you long to know.
Clutch the iron—heat it hot—
Be of spirit—falter not.
Like its glow shall be your Day;
Work with will, and work away!

III.

Mighty molder, hist and ho!
  Down there in your earthly halls,
Like the metal all aglow,
  How the sweat from off you falls—
Dripping with each heave or stroke,
As the rain drips from the oak!
Still the mold you well prepare—
Still the molten metal bear—
Still the casting comes out true:
Mighty molder, it will do!
Only when the eve shall lay
Aside the labors of the day,
And unto your wife you've come,
Sit not with her gloomy—dumb:
Look not sadly on her boys:
Dash not thus her matron joys:
Give to each and all a hope:
Strength and will with fate can cope.

As you bring the mass aglow,
You can bring or weal or woe;
As you mold or shaft or wheel,
You can mold or woe or weal.
You have strength to *make* the Day —
Work with will, then: work away!

IV.

Worn and weary workers—ho!
  Toil is pain, if so you say;
But to those who singing go
  To their labors day by day,
Toil is duty, growth and gain—
Never wasted—never vain.
Worker by the hot highway,
In the blinding blaze of day—
Delver in the deep, dark mine,
Where no rays of sunlight shine—
Patient, pent-up man-machine,
At the loom and shuttle seen,
Weaving in with nicest art
Throbbings of your own poor heart,
Till the subtle textures seem
With your very life to gleam—
Stitcher by the cradle's side,
Where thy fondest hopes abide,

Working with a heart of might
All the day, and half the night,
Sometimes till the east grows red
With the dawning, for thy bread,
Though thou art of feeble limb,
And thine eyes are pain'd and dim,
Sending off, with every piece
Which thy weary hands release,
Portions of thy life wrought in
With the garment white and thin—
Hard the task, but work away:
Yet shall dawn the Better Day.

V.

Faith is might, my brothers.   Ho!
   Weary workers everywhere,
For the New Age, rounding to
   Like a planet, now prepare:
Not by revel—not by rust—
Not by scorning yet your crust—
Not by idle dreams of wealth
Won by luck, or got by stealth—
Not by flattering hopes of ease:
Better, braver things than these,
As its first beams on you fall,
Asks the New Age of you all.

Workers! ye are brothers born—
Treat the title not with scorn.
Workers! born or where or when,
Better, ye are fellow-men:
Workers!—(so 'tis felt at length)—
Ye have got the gift of strength:
Yours the gift of numbers, too,
"Then what?" To yourselves be true!
Work with will, and work away,
Doubting not the Better Day!
Each to each a brother be—
Steadfast in your sympathy;
All to all be fellow-men;
Ye will lack but little then.
"We were made for Labor?" True,
So was labor made for you.
You are Labor's: Labor yours;
This your common weal secures.
Labor has been Money's long; .
And in this has been the wrong.
Let it hence be yours, and you
Labor's. Then, with duty due,
And with muscles well combin'd
With your energies of mind,
Workers! ye shall *masters* be
In the halls of Industry.

Heart and hope! The night withdrawn,
How the coming morn shall dawn!
Work, my brothers—work away,
Doubting not the Better Day!

VI.

"Heart and hope!" my brothers. Ho!
   Sons of sorrow, sons of toil,
Ye shall not forever go
   Yoked, as now—another's spoil.
See! the night is nearly pass'd,
And the morning dawns at last.
Far behind, the shadows lie
Dark against the troubled sky;
While, before, the arch is gray
Where the harbinger of day,
Rounding up the azure cope,
Flames the Morning Star of Hope.
—Be not hasty, be not rash,
Though its beams around you flash:
Time his offspring will mature—
Work and wait—the end is sure.
Falter not, but bide your time:
Calm endurance is sublime.
—Weary workers! work away:
God will lead the Better Day!

All Things Free.

———

FREE as the air, free as the sea,
Let all things come, let all things be:
The air, at every start and pause,
That still confesses natural laws—
· The sea, that ever ebbs and flows,
And still the laws of nature knows.

Free as that air's sky-cleaving bird,
Whose songs at Heav'ns blue gates are heard
Ere sunbeams tip earth's loftiest peak,
Let all things move, let all things speak—
For laws divine or human reach,
Or may, and wisely govern each.

Free as the sea's careering ships,
Whose arrowy speed the wind outstrips,
As o'er the broad and boundless deep,
Unaw'd, unchain'd, *but helm'd*, they sweep,
Let all things be, as all things can—
And first, and chief of all things, MAN.

Be Firm!—Be True!

———

. . . "As the sun,
Ere it has risen, sometimes paints its image
In the atmosphere, so often do the spirits*
Of great events stride on before the events—
And in to-day already walks to-morrow.'
SCHILLER—"*Wallenstein.*"

———

STATESMAN! on the giddy height
Whence, at will, thou swayest men,
Steals a darkness o'er thy sight?
Moves a cloud within thy ken?
Be firm!—Be true!
And though the hurtling heav'ns grow black,
Unfailing light shall gild thy track.

Orator! amid the crowd
Moved like waves at thy behest,
Hear'st thou that which, shouted loud,
Were a terror to thy breast?

———

* Nativism: exclusion—Foreign influence: home Catholicism: anti-popery—Papal pretensions: protestant intolerance—Ultra democracy: aristocratic republicanism.

Be firm!—Be true!
Then fall what may upon thine ear,
Thy heart shall feel no coward fear.

Christian! of the faith of Rome!
    Do you hear a hissing scorn
Rising 'gainst you, in the home
    Of your new-adoption born?
        Be firm!—Be true!
If God is with you, what care ye
Though hate roar as a raging sea?

Christian! of the faith that laid
    Rome's old bondage in the dust!
Fear'st thou that thou art betray'd?
    Feel'st thou that this quarrel's just?
        Be firm!—Be true!
Fall if it must be in the strife,
But yield not thou one inch for life!

Stranger! from a clime abroad,
    From a land beyond the sea,
Deem'st thou in thy heart that God
    Gives a home-right here to thee?
        Be firm!—Be true!
And though it cost thee all thou hast,
Assert that right while life shall last.

Freeman! born upon the soil!
　Fully, fairly, deemest thou
Alien arts would make a spoil
　Of this land of freedom now:
　　　Be firm!—Be true!
Resolve on what will shield from harm,
And *do it* with no laggard arm!

MAN! of every clime and creed!
　With a high and holy trust,
Dost thou on thy mission speed,
　Seeking but the Right, the Just?
　　　Be firm!—Be true!
Though sorely tried in many a way,
Despair not!—God will bring thy Day.

Spring Verses.

How with the song of every bird,
　And with the scent of every flow'r,
Some recollection dear is stirr'd
　Of many a long-departed hour,
Whose course, though shrouded now in night,
Was traced in lines of golden light!

I know not if, when years have cast
　Their shadows on life's early dreams,
'T is wise to touch the Hope that's past,
　And re-illume its fading beams:
But, though the future hath its star,
That olden Hope is dearer far.

Of all the present, much is bright;
　And in the coming years, I see
A brilliant and a cheering light,
　Which burns before me constantly,—
Guiding my steps, through haze and gloom,
To where Fame's turrets proudly loom.

Yet coldly shines it on my brow ;
   And in my breast it wakes to life
None of the holy feelings now,
   With which my boyhood's heart was rife :
It can not touch that secret spring
Which erst made life so bless'd a thing.

Give me—then give me birds and flow'rs,
   Which are the voice and breath of Spring !
For those the songs of life's young hours
   With thrilling touch recall and sing,—
And these, with their sweet breath, impart
Old tales, whose memory warms the heart.

To an Early Spring Flower.

———

First of the fruitful Springtime! welcome thou,
Beautiful pioneer of the Floral World!
As the bright, high-soul'd ones of human kind,
Go forth into the boundless wilderness
Fearless and first; and on the trackless deep,
Adventurous, dare the surge which ne'er before
Has curl'd and crested to the streaming flag;
The while unmindful of their toils severe,
And perils that encompass them: So thou,
Herald of after-coming multitudes,
Darest the chill and blighting storms of March,
And spread'st thy cheerful petals to the eye,
Regardless of the cloud that, stooping low,
Frowns darkly on thee, and with muttered threat
Spreads its thick folds between thee and the sun.

To me, dear art thou, herald flower! No rich,
And gaudy coloring, hast thou: thy leaves
Have not the rainbow-brightness, nor the deep
And dazzling hue of those which throng the earth
In summer, to the hot and burning sun

Opening their bosoms: But thou hast a tint
More delicate by far; and to the eye
Pleased with the simply beautiful, thou art
More grateful than the gaudily attired.
E'en as the beautiful of human-kind,
Who live not in the blaze of Fashion's sun,
Nor waste their early years at Folly's shrine,
—Where Nature's glorious handiwork is warp'd—
Are by the good of earth respected most,
And pleasantest to the All-seeing Eye.

Dandelions.

My heart leaps like a child's, when first
  I see them on their lowly stem,
As from still wint'ry fields they burst,
  Bright as the blue skies over them,
Sprinkling with gold the meadowy green,
Where Spring's approach is earliest seen.

They come in changeful April days,
  These children of the cloud and sun,
When light with shadow softly plays,
  As both along the ridges run,
Wooing the bee from out his cell,
With tales of flowery slopes they tell.

Bright horologe of seasons—they
  Proclaim the floral calends here,
Revealing when in woods away
  Spring flowers and singing birds appear,
Through open aisle and mazy bout
To lure the feet of childhood out.

I love them that so soon they spring
   Where slopes the meadow to the brook;
I love them that to earth they bring
   So cheerful and so warm a look;
And that again they give to me
The playmates of my infancy.

O! days of love, and trust, and truth;
   (The morning sky is strangely bright!)
O! loved companions of my youth;
   (How darkly closes in the night!)
Again the fields spread free and far;
Beyond them, still the woodlands are.

I'm with you now, glad-hearted ones!
   Where'er beneath the April sky
The flashing rill in music runs,
   Or flowery lawns in sunlight lie—
Where harvest apples ripe we see,
And where the summer berries be.

I'm with you where the cardinal bird
   Pipes in the budding groves of spring,
And where the thrasher's song is heard
   Till all the summer forests ring;
Where nuts in autumn fall, and where
The wild grape hangs, I'm with you there.

O! days of love, and trust, and truth;
   (The flowers were bright upon the lawn!)
O! loved companions of my youth;
   (How many, like the flowers, are gone!)
Nor flower nor child goes down in vain:
Ye both shall rise and bloom again.

May.

———

WOULD that thou couldst last for aye,
Merry, ever-merry May!
Made of sun-gleams, shade and showers,
Bursting buds, and breathing flowers!
Dripping-lock'd, and rosy-vested,
Violet-slipper'd, rainbow-crested;
Girdled with the eglantine,
Festoon'd with the dewy vine:
Merry, ever-merry May,
Would that thou couldst last for aye!

Out beneath thy morning sky!
Dian's bow still hangs on high!
And in the blue depths afar,
Glimmers, here and there, a solitary star.
Diamonds robe the bending grass,
   Glist'ning early flowers among—
Monad's world, and fairy's glass,
Bathing fount for wandering sprite—
   By mysterious fingers hung
In the lone and quiet night.
Now the freshening breezes pass—

Gathering, as they steal along,
Rich perfume, and matin song—
And quickly to destruction hurl'd
Is fairy's diamond glass, and monad's dewdrop
    world.
Lo! yon cloud, which hung but now
Black upon the mountain's brow,
Threatening the green earth with storm—
See! it heaves its giant form,
And, ever changing shape and hue,
But still presenting something new,
Moves slowly up, and spreading rolls away
Toward the rich purple streaks that usher in
    the day;
Bright'ning, as it onward goes,
Until its very center glows
With the warm, cheering light, the coming sun
    bestows:
As the passing Christian's soul,
Nearing the celestial goal,
Bright and brighter grows, till God illumes the
    whole.

Out beneath thy noontide sky!
On a shady slope I lie,
    Giving fancy ample play;

And there 's not more blest than I,
  One of Adam's race to-day.
Out beneath thy noontide sky!
Earth, how beautiful!—how clear
Of cloud or mist the atmosphere!
What a glory greets the eye!
What a calm, or quiet stir,
Steals o'er Nature's worshiper—
Silent, yet so eloquent,
That we feel 't is heaven-sent—
Waking thoughts that long have slumber'd
Passion-dimm'd and earth-encumber'd—
Bearing soul and sense away,
To revel in the Perfect Day
That 'waits us, when we shall for aye
Discard this darksome dust—this prison-house
    of clay!

Out beneath thy evening sky!
Not a breeze that wanders by
But hath swept the green earth's bosom—
Rifling the rich grape-vine blossom,
Dallying with the simplest flower
In mossy nook and rosy bower—
To the perfum'd green-house straying,
And with rich exotics playing—

Then, unsated, sweeping over
Banks of thyme, and fields of clover!
Out beneath thy evening sky!
Groups of children caper by,
Crown'd with flowers, and rush along
With joyous laugh, and shout, and song.
Flashing eye, and radiant cheek,
Spirits all unsunn'd bespeak.
They are in Life's May-month hours—
And those wild bursts of joy, what are they but
  Life's flowers?

Would that thou could'st last for aye,
Merry, ever-merry May!
Made of sun-gleams, shade and showers,
Bursting buds, and breathing flowers;
Dripping-lock'd, and rosy-vested,
Violet-slipper'd, rainbow-crested;
Girdled with the eglantine,
Festoon'd with the dewy vine:
Merry, ever-merry May,
Would that thou couldst last for aye!

The Cardinal Bird.

She brought a redbird in a cage
   And hung it from my window-sill :—
The redbird then was all the rage,
     And may be still.
I know not—I so long have been
Amid the city's dust and din.
But when I was a little child
I greatly loved its wood-notes wild,
Which lured me many a sunny day
Through maple-forests far away.
For years though I had seldom heard
    The cardinal bird.

A day and then a week pass'd by :—
   The redbird hanging from the sill
Sang not; and all were wondering why
     It was so still—
When one bright morning, loud and clear,
Its whistle smote my drowsy ear,
Ten times repeated, till the sound
Fill'd every echoing niche around;

And all things earliest loved by me,
—The bird, the brook, the flower, the tree,—
Came back again, as thus I heard
    The cardinal bird.

Where maple orchards towered aloft,
  And spicewood bushes spread below,
Where skies were blue, and winds were soft,
    I could but go—
For, opening through a wildering haze,
Appeared my restless childhood's days;
And truant feet and loitering mood
Soon found me in the same old wood,
  —(Illusion's hour but seldom brings
  So much the very form of things)—
Where first I sought, and saw, and heard
    The cardinal bird.

Then came green meadows, broad and bright,
  Where dandelions, with wealth untold,
Gleam'd on the young and eager sight
    Like stars of gold—
And on the very meadow's edge,
Beneath the ragged blackberry hedge,
'Mid mosses golden, gray and green,
The fresh young butter-cups were seen,

And small spring-beauties, sent to be
The heralds of Anemone:
All just as when I earliest heard
　　　The cardinal bird.

Upon the gray old forest's rim
　　I snuff'd the crab-tree's sweet perfume;
. And farther, where the light was dim,
　　　I saw the bloom
Of May-apples, beneath the tent
Of umbrel leaves above them bent:
Where oft was shifting light and shade
The blue-eyed ivy wildly stray'd;
And Solomon's-seal, in graceful play,
Swung where the straggling sunlight lay:—
The same as when I earliest heard
　　　The cardinal bird.

And on the slope, above the rill
　　That wound among the sugar-trees,
I heard them at their labors still,
　　　The murmuring bees:
Bold foragers! that come and go
Without permit from friend or foe:
In the tall tulip-trees o'er head
On pollen greedily they fed;

And from low purple phlox, that grew
About my feet, sipp'd honey-dew.
How like the scenes when first I heard
        The cardinal bird!

How like!—and yet . . . The spell grows
        weak :—
    Ah, but I miss the sunny brow—
The sparkling eye—the ruddy cheek!
        Where, where are now
The three who then beside me stood
Like sunbeams in the dusky wood?
Alas! I am alone.   Since then,
They've trod the weary ways of men :—
One on the eve of manhood died ;
Two in its flush of pow'r and pride.
Their graves are green, where first we heard
        The cardinal bird.

The redbird from the window hung,
    Not long my fancies thus beguiled :
Again in maple-groves it sung
        Its wood-notes wild ;
For, rousing with a tearful eye,
I gave it to the trees and sky.—

I miss'd so much those brothers three,
Who walk'd youth's flowery ways with me,
I could not, dared not, but believe
It too had brothers, that would grieve
Till in old haunts again 't was heard,
      The cardinal bird.

𝔄 𝔖𝔲𝔪𝔪𝔢𝔯 𝔖𝔠𝔢𝔫𝔢.

———

THE day was well nigh o'er;
The sun, near the horizon, dimly shone;
And the long shadows of the door-yard trees,
   Athwart the yard were thrown.
   Before our humble door,
   Upon the soft, cool grass,
With bosom open to the evening breeze
   Which now and then did pass,
Musing, and dreaming of the spirit's birth,
And its relations to this beautiful earth,
   I lay alone—
Borne on Imagination's airy pinions,
Far from the world's turmoil, and sordid man's dominions.

Eve came on gently : and her step was seen
Stirring the blossoms on the velvet green,
   And warning home the laden bee,
    Yet laboring busily.
    The while, her soft
And delicate fingers pluck'd the leaves aloft,

And whirl'd them round and round
In eddies to the ground,
Where I, an humble PAN, with many a wreath was crown'd!

Presently on my ear,
Rang full and deep,
Joyous, and musical, and clear,
A sound, which made my father-heart to leap,
And sent the quick blood to my cheek and brow,
Which with the recollection warm e'en now.
It ceased, that thrilling tone:
And with it passed my bright but dreamy train
Of thought—and I was but a man again,
Earthly, and weak, and lone.
So slight a touch can jar the spirit's springs—
And e'en a word, or tone, or look, clip Fancy's wings.

Once more—Once more, it rang upon my ear—
But blent with other sounds, as clear
And musical as it:
A childish jest—and then a shout,
From one, or two, or three, rang out,
Full, free, and wild—
And then a fit
Of childish laughter rent the dewy air!
And now my eye a glimpse caught of the fair

And lovely ONE: It was my own dear child!
She and her little friends, hard at their play,
Upon the grassy slope, that softly stretch'd away.

Again—again—
From the descending plain,
Up rise those gleeful notes: but chief that voice
Which first broke on my ear,
And made my heart rejoice,
Ascends, full, strong, and clear—
Approaching nigh and nigher,
As the strain grows high and higher;
Then, like a water-circle, flowing
Away to every point, and growing
Fainter, and fainter, till the last tones die,
Lost, as far-journeying birds fade in the purple sky.

Bonnets were in the air,
And bonnet-ribbands scattered on the ground;
Small shoes and pantalettes lay thick around,
And tiny feet were bare:
And frocks were soil'd, and aprons rent;
But still they kept their frolic-mood,
And laugh'd and romp'd; and when I went
And closer by them stood,

How hard each little elf did try
    To win the most of my regard;
Now gazing anxious in my eye,
    And striving still more hard:
The spirit, so it seem'd to me,
The same in the great world we see,
Spurring the warrior on to victory,
    And urging on the bard:
Each had success as much at heart,
As he who plays in war or politics his part.

    "My child!—my child!"
  She comes to me:
Her cheeks are flush'd, her hair is wild,
    Her pulse is bounding free:
    With laugh and shout she comes—but see!
    Half way she stops, as still as death;
Her look is sad—she hardly draws a breath.
    "My child! my own dear child!
    Tell me, what aileth thee?"
"Father!"—she pointed to the moon,
On the horizon's shatter'd bound—
    'T was rising, full and round.
    "Father! I'm coming soon."
Her other hand now pointed to the West,
Where the dim sun was sinking to his rest.

"Father! are those the eyes of God
Looking upon us here?"
Her knee bent slowly to the dewy sod—
And then came tear on tear:
A gush of mingled feeling—wonder, and joy, and fear.

The Mountain Paths.

———

COME to the hills with me!
Come tread the cool and flow'r-gem'd paths, that wind
    'Neath many a stately tree—
    Trees that for aye have lined
The airy summits of our Western Land:
The stars are fading, and the air is bland.

    Come to the hills with me!
The fresh-lipp'd Morn is breathing glorious life:
    Don thy calash, and flee
    The city's dust and strife;
Leave thy prunelle, and silken hose,—and take
Cotton and calf-skin!—quick, thy toilet make!

    Here—take the garden's pride!
Thy cheek, like it, will soon be rosy-fair.
    Now for the green hill side,
    And the pure upland air!
Death floats in every breeze that fans us here—
Oh, for the cottage of the mountaineer!

So—we are winding up;
The fair stars have not all yet left the sky:
    There—pluck that honey-cup!
    Thy slender hand will vie
With it in whiteness; and—but I forget—
Dark eyes compare not with the violet:

    Still, pluck it too; I'll call
Thine bright as any star, in any place.
    Nay—let thy bonnet fall
    Back from thy radiant face!
Heart's-ease, anemone, shrub, rose-of-May;
——Whither thine eyes now? Ah! the King of Day!

    Gloriously comes he there!
Morn on the hills! One hour of life like this,
    Pays for whole weeks of care;
    Earth scarce hath greater bliss:
Yet "angel visits" are almost as many
As visits to the hills—*They turn no penny!*

    What life is this I feel?
A new sensation thrills through every vein:
    And glowing fancies steal
    Athwart my wondering brain:
Visions of Eld—hopes—aspirations—fears
That vanish soon—bright dreams of coming years!

'Neath these old oaks and elms,
The spirit hath a fullness of delight—
 A depth of joy, that whelms,
 Like the lone, starry night,
Our intellectual being, in a maze,
Where fancy, pleas'd, bewilder'd, startled, plays—

 Now floundering in gloom,
Now reveling in glory, as a ray
 The darkness doth illume:
 Then bursts the perfect day,
And the clear'd vision wanders wide and free
Through the starr'd realms of vast Infinity.

 Morn on the hill-tops! Hark!
The low of kine swells up from yon green vale,
 With song of meadow-lark,
 And merry note of quail;
And the "hip-halloo!" of the wild cow-boy,
Comes, soft and musical, and full of joy.

 The breeze is rising now:
The purple clouds sail gracefully along;
 The spiral saplings bow,
 And swell the choral song;
And from each tree-top, by the free wind stirr'd,
Floats the rich matin of some grateful bird.

20

Man—man alone! of all
To whom this visible glory hath been given,
Deemeth the privilege small
Thus to commune with Heaven:
There is no bank or railroad stock on high—
Stars are not gold—pence rain not from the sky!

A Harvest Hymn.

GREAT GOD!—our heart-felt thanks to Thee!
  We feel thy presence everywhere;
And pray, that we may ever be
  Thus objects of thy guardian care.

We sow'd!—by Thee our work was seen,
  And bless'd; and instantly went forth
Thy mandate; and in living green
  Soon smiled the fair and fruitful earth.

We toil'd!—and Thou didst note our toil;
  And gav'st the sunshine and the rain,
Till ripen'd on the teeming soil
  The fragrant grass, and golden grain.

And now, we reap!—and oh, our God!
  From this, the earth's unbounded floor,
We send our Song of Thanks abroad,
  And pray Thee, bless our hoarded store!

August.

Dust on thy mantle! dust,
Bright summer, on thy livery of green!
A tarnish, as of rust,
Dims thy late-brilliant sheen:
And thy young glories—leaf, and bud, and flower—
Change cometh over them with every hour.

Thee hath the August sun
Look'd on with hot, and fierce, and brassy face;
And still and lazily run,
Scarce whispering in their pace,
The half-dried rivulets, that lately sent
A shout of gladness up, as on they went.

Flame-like, the long mid-day,
With not so much of sweet air as hath stirr'd
The down upon the spray,
Where rests the panting bird,
Dozing away the hot and tedious noon,
With fitful twitter, sadly out of tune.

Seeds in the sultry air,
And gossamer web-work on the sleeping trees;
E'en the tall pines, that rear
Their plumes to catch the breeze,
The slightest breeze from the unfreshening west,
Partake the general languor and deep rest.

Happy as man may be,
Stretch'd on his back, in homely bean-vine bower,
While the voluptuous bee
Robs each surrounding flower,
And prattling childhood clambers o'er his breast,
The husbandman enjoys his noonday rest.

Against the hazy sky,
The thin and fleecy clouds unmoving rest:
Beneath them far, yet high
In the dim, distant west,
The vulture, scenting thence its carrion-fare,
Sails, slowly circling in the sunny air.

Soberly, in the shade,
Repose the patient cow, and toil-worn ox;
Or in the shoal stream wade,
Shelter'd by jutting rocks;
The fleecy flock, fly-scourged and restless, rush
Madly from fence to fence, from bush to bush.

Tediously pass the hours,
And vegetation wilts, with blister'd root—
  And droop the thirsting flowers,
  Where the slant sun-beams shoot;
But of each tall old tree, the lengthening line,
Slow-creeping eastward, marks the day's decline.

Faster, along the plain,
Moves now the shade, and on the meadow's edge:
  The kine are forth again,
  Birds flitter in the hedge.
Now in the molten west sinks the hot sun:
Welcome, mild eve!—the sultry day is done.

Pleasantly comest thou,
Dew of the evening, to the crisp'd-up grass;
  And the curl'd corn-blades bow,
  As the light breezes pass,
That their parch'd lips may feel thee, and expand,
Thou sweet reviver of the fevered land.

So, to the thirsting soul,
Cometh the dew of the Almighty's love;
  And the scathed heart, made whole,
  Turneth in joy above,
To where the spirit freely made expand,
And rove, untrammel'd, in that "better land."

Happiness—A Picture.

A GREEN vale, and an humble cot
    Embowered in vines and spreading trees;
Before the door a verdant plot,
    And flowers whose perfume loads the breeze:
Upon the grass, those flowers among,
    Glad as the winds that thither stray,
A group of children, fair and young,—
    Their cheeks are flush'd with play!

Midway the two small rooms between,
    (For only two hath cot like this,)
Spectator of the joyous scene,
    And sharer of the heart-felt bliss,
A white-haired grandam;—on her knee
    Her knitting lies neglected now;
She fairly strains her eyes to see,—
    Her spees pushed to her brow!

A smile upon her withered cheeks,—
    On each a glistening tear-drop lies;
Her lips apart—she thoughtless speaks,
    And harder strains her filmy eyes.

An anguish'd cry!—she quickly sprung,—
　　The sufferer's head was on her breast;
A bee its tiny foot had stung,
　　On clover-blossom prest.

Autumn Afternoon.

In the clouds my eye makes pictures,
 And paints them on the sky,
And I photograph them on my mind
 As they go drifting by.

In the air my ear finds music,
 And tracks it to the trees,
And I score it on my heart before
 It leaves me with the breeze.

On the earth my heart hears voices
 From the buried whom I love,
And I lean to listen, but I find
 Them echoes from Above.

On the seas my spirit trembles
 At the wierd, wild tones it hears,
But it's only waves, I know, that sing
 The Anthem of the Years.

From deep valleys, looking upward,
 All is calm that I descry,

21

But I know the earth is fill'd with strife
  Beneath that quiet sky.

On the mountains, gazing downward,
  Of my heav'nward height I'm vain,
Yet I know the earth, seen from above,
  Is all one level plain.

And it's always thus :—wherever
  I go, whatever do,
Still the False is sure to come with strength,
  But stronger comes the True.

And the False comes first in order,
  Its face all wreath'd with smiles,
And thus tempts me with its hollowness,
  And woos me with its wiles.

But I think me of the temple,
  And the pinnacle of old—
Of the False that shrank with terror there,
  And the True that there were bold.

And I think of the high mountain,
  And the wealth that lay in view—
And the Devil there that still was false,
  And the Christ that still was True.

And I think me of the Angels
 In the paths of Space that trod,
And there minister'd, in light and love,
 To Him, the Son of God.

And I think of all the Shadows
 That, like night, make dim my way,
But pass off, or soon or late, and leave
 The certain light of day;

And of all the blessèd angels
 That these shades have broken through,
With their constant warnings of the False,
 And their whispers of the True.

Then I send a voice to Heaven,
 With my thanks for every boon;
And I worry not—but still enjoy
 My Autumn Afternoon.

To a Late Fall Flower.

RICH, golden-hued, and fair!
Beautiful gem 'mid the surrounding blight!
　　Cheerfully wav'st thou there,
　　A blessing to the sight:
And lavishly dost thou thy sweets dispense—
A balmy pleasure to the longing sense.

　　When the fair buds of spring
Have burst, and bloom'd, and faded from the eye,
　　And the rich blossoming
　　Of summer hath pass'd by,
Thou com'st, 'mid chilling sleet, and winds that blight,
Gladdening the gloom—a star in Sorrow's night.

　　Thus, when youth's smooth, and fair,
And rose-leaf tinted cheek hath pass'd away;
　　And the rich, glossy hair,
　　Is dim, and thin, and grey;
And Time's fierce storms, and Age's wintry wind,
Have scathed the body, and just spared the mind;

Then, 'mid the general gloom,
Bursts forth a light to guide the weary on,
   Joyfully, to the tomb,
   Where life's long march is done:
Light of the soul! that from its heavenly height
Dispels the darkness of the gathering night.

The Wreck at Sea.

———

THE sun was low—a flood of light
　　Slept on the glittering ocean—
And Night's dark robes were journeying up,
　　With slow and solemn motion:
And ever-and-anon was heard
The sea-mew's shriek—ill-omened bird!

Down sunk the sun—the gathering mist
　　Rose proudly up before it,
And streamed upon the lurid air,
　　A blood-red banner o'er it:
Frowning, and piled up heap on heap,
Dense clouds o'erspread the mighty Deep;
Darker, and pitchy black they grew—
And rolled, and wheeled, and onward flew,
　　Like marshaling of men.
Then trembled timid souls with fear—
Glistened in beauty's eye the tear—
And "fatherland" was doubly dear—
　　But brave hearts quailed not *then*.

Soon the rough tar's prophetic eye
Saw many a floating shroud on high,
And many a coffin drifting by—
   And on the driving gale
Beheld the spirits of the Deep,
Above—around—in fury sweep—
   Then he heard a low, sad wail,
   And at times a muttered curse,
As on the fierce and troubled wind,
Rode Death—and, following close behind,
   A dark and sombre hearse.
And soon the barque a wreck was driven,
Before the free, wild winds of heaven!
Now shrank with fear each gallant heart—
   Bended was many a knee—
And the last prayer was offered up
   God of the Deep, to Thee!
Muttered the angry heavens still,
   And murmured still the sea—
And old and sterner hearts bowed down,
   God of the Deep, to Thee!
And still the wreck was onward driven,
   Upon the wide, wild sea—
And MAN's proud soul to Fate was given,
   WOMAN's, oh God, to Thee!

Gaped wide the Deep—down plunged the wreck—
    Up rose a fearful yell—
Death's wings flapped o'er that sinking deck—
    A shudder!— all was still.

To My Mother.

———

Thy cheek—it is pale my mother,
   And the light of thine eye is dim—
And the gushings of gladness, that used to fill
   Thy cup of joy to its brim,
Come like the visits of angels,
   So "few and far between,"
That I feel the reed is a feeble one
   On which thou hence must lean.

'Tis a bitter thing, my mother,
   To look on a parent's decay—
To behold the Spoiler's ravages,
   As he tears life's bloom away:
'Tis bitter to look on the furrows
   He ploughs in the thoughtful brow—
To weep o'er the gems of intellect
   That are rayless, and sheenless now.

But there is a thought, my mother,
   That is balm to the stricken heart:

—Though the gift of life is a frail one,
    And from it we soon must part,
There is a haven of gladness,
    For the weary heart a home,
Where the light of joy is never dim,
    And sorrows never come.

On that blissful home, my mother,
    Thine eye is often bent,
Like a tiny child's on a wished-for-thing—
    So longing—so intent.
Oh, how pure in the eye of Heaven
    Must the heart of the Christian be—
So entirely fixed on that home above,
    From earthliness so free!

The Bridal.

He stood before the altar; and a shade
Of darkness for a moment crossed his brow,
And melted into beauty on his lip;
And a slight tremor thrilled him, as the blood
Came boiling to his forehead—and sunk back,
And rushed tumultuous to his burning cheek.
But this was over—and the confidence
Of manhood was upon him; and he stood
Erect, in pride and nobleness, before
The minister of the High God—a man
Hoary and tremulous, and bowed with years.
And she, the loved, the beautiful, stood up
Beside the chosen one; and meekly bent
Her half-closed eyes upon her swelling breast:
And on her temples slept a raven tress,
Shading her beautiful veins, that melted through,
Like amethyst half-hidden in the snow.
And loveliness hung round her, like a soft
And silvery drapery.   And pain, and sin,
And sorrow's discipline, on her fair brow
Had no abiding place.   The various shades

Of sorrow and of gladness, came and went
With almost every pulse, like the uncertain
And silent memory of forgotten dreams.
They stood together—and their hearts were proud,
His of its nobleness, *and hers of him!*
The holy father offered up a prayer,
That happiness in after time might be
The guerdon of their love—and that the star
Which rose so beautiful and cloudless now,
Might light their years of trial, and go down
Calmly, as it arose—and they were ONE.

Here endeth this fair picture.   Time wore on,
And they commingled with the callous world,
And had their day of glory and of gloom,
And slept and were forgotten.   Others came,
And filled their places at the social hearth:
They too have passed away.   And ever thus
Time silently goes on his ceaseless round,
Unnoticed and unknown; and human kind
Are but the puppets, moved about at will,
And lain within the dreamless sepulcher,
To wait the coming of that far-off day,
When the enfranchised spirit shall awake,
And burst the cerements of the humid grave,
And live, and be immortal!

𝕭𝖆𝖗𝖑𝖊𝖞 𝕭𝖗𝖊𝖊.

———

In Auld Scotia was thy home,
  Barley Bree! Barley Bree!
But thou sawest fit to roam
  O'er the sea :—
And thy roving feet have trod
Wheresoe'er the smile of God
Hath lent greenness to the sod
  Barley Bree.

Thou hast been a jovial wight,
  Barley Bree! Barley Bree!
Ever ready, day or night,
  With thy glee ;
And as time has sped along,
'Midst thy laugh, and joke, and song,
Thou hast never dream'd of wrong,
  Barley Bree.

Thy heart was ever warm,
  Barley Bree! Barley Bree!
If sunshine or if storm
  Came to thee,

And the poor who sought thy door,
Though oft helped by thee before,
Ever freely shared thy store,
   Barley Bree!

Thou didst alway love thy drop,
   Barley Bree! Barley Bree!
But the pint at which to stop,
   Thou did'st see.
Yet the habit grew too strong,
And thou lingeredst too long
O'er the draught and o'er the song,
   Barley Bree!

And as time flew round about,
   Barley Bree! Barley Bree!
Thine own elbow soon peeped out,
   And thy knee;
And thy face grew round and red,
And thy jollity all fled,
And the street was oft thy bed,
   Barley Bree!

But an angel help'd thee up,
   Barley Bree! Barley Bree!
And for aye the poison-cup
   Thou did'st flee;

And again thou art erect,
And with mirth thy brow is deck'd,
And thou hast the world's respect,
   Barley Bree.

The Revelers.

————

THERE were sounds of mirth and revelry,
In an old ancestral hall,
And many a merry laugh rang out,
And many a merry call;
And the glass was freely pass'd around,
And the red wine freely quaff'd;
And many a heart beat high with glee,
And the joy of the thrilling draught—
    In that broad and huge ancestral hall,
    Of the times that were, of old.

A voice arose, as the lights grew dim,
And a glass was flourished high:
"I drink to Life!" said a Reveler bold,
"And I do not fear to die.
I have no fear—I have no fear—
Talk not of the vagrant, Death;
For he's but a grim old gentleman,
And wars but with his breath."
    A boast well worthy a revel-rout
    Of the times that were, of old.

"We drink," said all, " We drink to Life
And we do not fear to die!"
Just then a rushing sound was heard,
As of quick wings sweeping by;
And soon the old latch was lifted up,
And the door flew open wide,
And a stranger strode within the hall,
With an air of martial pride:
  In visor and cloak, like a secret knight
  Of the times that were, of old.

He spoke: "I join in your revelry,
Bold sons of the Bacchan rite,
And I drink the toast ye have filled to drink,
The pledge of yon dauntless knight:
Fill high—fill higher—we drink to Life,
And we scorn the vagrant, Death,
For he's but a grim old gentleman,
And wars but with his breath."
  A pledge well worthy a revel-rout
  Of the times that were, of old.

"He's a noble soul, that champion knight,
And he wears a martial brow:
Oh, he'll pass the gates of Paradise,
To the regions of bliss below!"

17

The Reveler stood in deep amaze—
Now flashed his fiery eye;
He muttered a curse—then shouted loud,
"Intruder, thou shalt die!"
 And his sword leap'd out, like a baron's brave,
 Of the times that were, of old.

He struck—and the stranger's guise fell off,
When a phantom before him stood,
A grinning, and ghastly, and horrible thing,
That curdled his boiling blood.
He stirred not again, till the stranger blew
A blast of his withering breath;
Then the Reveler fell at the Phantom's feet,
And his conqueror was—DEATH!
 In that broad and high ancestral hall,
 Of the times that were, of old.

The Invalid.

SHE came in Spring, when leaves were green,
　　And birds sang blithe in bower and tree,
A stranger, but her gentle mien
　　It was a calm delight to see.
In every motion, grace was hers;
　　On every feature, sweetness dwelt;
Thoughts soon became her worshipers—
　　Affections soon before her knelt.

She bloom'd through all the summer days
　　As sweetly as the fairest flowers,
And till October's softening haze
　　Came with its still and dreamy hours.
So calm the current of her life,
　　So lovely and serene its flow,
We hardly mark'd the deadly strife
　　Disease forever kept below.

But Autumn winds grew wild and chill,
　　And pierced her with their icy breath;
And when the snow on plain and hill
　　Lay white, she passed, and slept in death.

Tones only of immortal birth
  Our memory of her voice can stir;
With things too beautiful for earth
  Alone do we remember her.

She came in Spring, when leaves were green,
  And birds sang blithe in bower and tree,
And flowers sprang up and bloomed between
  Low branches and the quickening lea.
The greenness of the leaf is gone,
  The beauty of the flower is riven,
The birds to other climes have flown,
  And there's an angel more in Heaven.

A Wonderful Story.

I.

Last night, in the deep mid watches,
  As I sat alone in my room,
A Form stood suddenly by me,
  That at first seem'd part of the gloom,—
But anon, by the few, faint embers,
  Distinct all its outlines grew,
And I saw that the gloom of my chamber,
  And the gloom of the Form, were two.

II.

Ere long the defined proportions
  Of a gray old man stood there,
Looking out from his beard of silver,
  And his thin, white, flowing hair.
His face, in its whole expression,
  Was beautiful and benign,
As he leant his staff in the corner,
  And took a seat by mine.

III.

Then the gloom in my chamber vanish'd;
  And the light,—it so did seem,—

Came out from his shadowy vestments,
  In many a flash and stream.
And soon, through the thin, pale ashes,
  Appear'd a tortuous flame;
And the characters which it pictured,
  Were the letters of a name.

IV.

And that name was simply—WISDOM:
  But why or whence it came,
I learnt not from the ashes—
  I learnt not from the flame.
But the old man entertain'd me
  With a story that was new;
And in its clear unwindings
  Perhaps may lie the clew:—

V.

VI.

I know no more about it,
   Than what I hear unfold:
Thus the Greybeard sought my chamber—
   This the story that he told;
But I've often thought, ISOLA,
   If the tales told you and me
Were more of them like this one,
   How much better it would be.

Thirty=Five.

———

THE keystone of the arch of Life, is now
    Beneath me. Thoughtfully I hence survey
What is to be, and what has been, and bow
    My head in deep humility, and lay
My pride in dust, that with my willing mind,
    And with my vigorous arm, and with my heart
As strong, I've done so little for my kind,
    And less for God . . . Here Life's two eras part:
The past, MY past, I count but little worth:
I've fell'd the forest, broken up the earth,
And gathered here a seed, and there a root,
Of flower, and grain, and berry-bearing shoot;
But all was purpose—preparation—plan—
The small beginnings of Life's little span.
The FUTURE of my being is for toil:—
To plant the gathered germs, and till the soil,
And, without indolence or weak surcease,
Watch the quick growth, and help the large increase;
Then, as Life's circling seasons onward move,
    To heap the bounteous summer's golden grain,
      And autumn's fruitage, on the lumbering wain.
Grant me, Thou Mighty One who sitt'st above,
To sow the seeds of Truth, and reap the fruits of Love.

FINIS.

www.ingramcontent.com/pod-product-compliance
Lightning Source LLC
Chambersburg PA
CBHW030638030726
47497CB00006B/1846